Overcoming The Fear Within

A Guide to Freedom Through God's Word

Randy Schroeder

Published by
Gateway to Freedom Publications
A division of Gateway to Freedom
P.O. Box 530143
Livonia, MI 48153-0143
ISBN: 0-9741805-3-X

For current information about Gateway to Freedom and Gateway to Freedom Publications visit our web site:

http://www.gatewaytofreedom.org

Cover photography by Gerald R. Schroeder
Printed in Lima, Peru by RS Print

Acknowledgements:

I would like to express my gratitude to my immediate family and special friends who have helped in this endeavor. Not only have these dearly loved ones shown the love of Jesus in my times of testing and overcoming, but they gave their time and talents in the task of proof reading this book. Thank you.

I would also like to acknowledge the inspiration and ministry of Pastor Henry W. Wright of Pleasant Valley Church in Thomaston, Georgia. Pastor Wright's ministry is noted for ministering healing to all and especially those deemed "incurable." He has had a high degree of success in bringing God's healing to those suffering with more than six hundred diseases. References made are for use of material from Pastor Henry's book titled, "A More Excellent Way, his recorded tapes about "Fear" and the forty hour teaching titled, "For my Life." His teaching series have given me considerable enlightenment to the medical aspects of the mind, body, spirit connection.

Henry W. Wright, Pleasant Valley Church, Inc., 4178 Highway 74 West
Thomaston, GA 30286, Ph: 1-800-453-5775

Dedication

This book is dedicated to my wife for all of the encouragement she has given to me in its writing and throughout my times of greatest trials. In the times of my greatest spiritual and physical torment and testing, she stood in prayer and faith. She not only "prayed through," but has served as chief editor to bring a greater simplicity and understanding to the text. Only the woman given by God to be my helpmate could have fulfilled all the roles required of her.

Table of Contents:

Table of Contents:

Introduction:

The alarm clock showed 3:45 AM as I abruptly awoke with my ears ringing and my body trembling to the ominous feeling of evil. The hairs on the back of my neck and arm stood straight out as I sensed the approach of something I couldn't see. I tried to reason that this had to be my imagination triggered by my utter exhaustion from the depression, sleepless nights and pain in my sides. But this wasn't the first time, and then my torso began quivering without control as the stomach acid built up in my burning throat. The evil came closer and closer until the pain shot through me like I'd been hit with a high powered electric shock. I threatened, commanded and cried out for the help of Jesus, but was overcome with fear as I was wracked with pain and torment.

While the preceding account may sound like the screenplay for a horror movie, I assure you that this happened to me – again and again for nearly two years as the Lord opened my understanding. Medical practitioners and religious leaders generally agree that the three most common and traumatic shocks we can receive are the death of a loved one, divorce, and the loss of a job. These and other traumatic events trigger the fears within us and if not resolved, cause a variety of physical, psychological and spiritual maladies. The manifestations listed above were but a few of the symptoms that came upon me after I had experienced the trauma of having my job eliminated at 53 years of age.

Generational heritages and unknown fears from my childhood and beyond were revealed under the purifying fire of God's testings. As you'll soon understand, I was tormented by two of the three primary ruling spirits of fear: the fear of man and the fear of death. These two principle fears include such fears as the fear of: identity loss, rejection, poverty, reproach, etc. As these fears became dominant over a long period of time, my immune system was compromised and my thinking impaired so that I was faced with even more fears like the fear of: insanity, debilitation, even greater illness, abandonment and many more.

Through this time of torment, God's Holy Spirit revealed how to overcome my fears and begin to begin walking in the newness of His revealed truth. The truths I share in this book will help you understand and overcome your fears as well. This is not an attempt to apply the principles of man's understanding, psychology or psychiatry. Although I have included some of my experiences, it is also not a diary, but rather a roadmap to freedom through the knowledge and practice of the revealed Word of God.

God's Word says that in the last days, great fear will cause men's hearts to fail. Some of these failing hearts will be among the very brethren who look forward to Jesus' second coming unless the bride of Christ will make herself ready. We don't have to be the victim of fear and perish for our lack of knowledge. Today, more than ever before, we need to search the scriptures to provide answers for our world and ourselves.

My prayer is that you would stop and ask Father God to anoint you and allow the Holy Spirit to be your teacher. As you read the pages that follow, I pray that He would open your understanding, enable you to embrace the truths of God's Word, and deliver you from all bondages of fear and the infirmities rooted therein. May God bless you and "may you prosper and be in health, even as thy soul prospers."

Randy Schroeder

Yea, if thou criest after knowledge, and liftest up thy voice for understanding: If thou seekest her as silver, and searchest for her as for hid treasures; Then shalt thou understand the fear of the LORD, and find the knowledge of God.
(Proverbs 2:3-5)

Chapter One

Two Types of Fear

For God hath not given us the spirit of fear; but of power, and of love, and of a sound mind.
(2 Timothy 1:7)

I was leisurely driving home from work one spring evening heading directly into the setting sun. It was after the rush hour, and a large, open tailgate truck was traveling in the far right lane nearly a hundred yards in front of me at the 70 MPH Interstate speed limit. Suddenly, I saw the truck bounce violently to its left side as it hit a particularly deep pothole caused by the winter icing. I began to steer over a lane to avoid the anticipated pothole when I saw the most surreal sight through the glare of the setting sun.

As if they were marching in a single column, three fifty-five gallon steel drums came sliding off the back of the truck one after the other! I instantly became fully alert, seeing every detail, as the first one landed upright and quickly spun on its rim into the ditch on my left. The second landed flat and rolled directly at me until it also went to my left about 30 yards in front of my car. However, the last one landed upright and began to spin and wobble in its race down the expressway. It first wobbled to the left. Just as I was about to steer to the right lane again, it also went right, then left, and right, again. I was looking at a fast closing barrel that seemingly anticipated every move that I thought to make. I felt trapped and unable to get out of its way! Finally, the barrel shot across the front of the car into the right ditch – missing me by only a few feet!

After I escaped the danger and passed the truck (which had pulled off the highway), I realized that my fingers were clamped to the steering wheel, exposing my white knuckles. My heart was racing. I was breathing rapidly. My arms quivered from the tension. My mouth suddenly felt dry and my neck and back were stiff. I exhaled a big breath of air, thanked the Lord for His protection and began to relax. By the time I reached home, my body had returned to more or less normal, even though my mouth continued to flap about this frightening experience for a day or so.

My state of alarm and its associated physiological responses were the result of what the dictionary describes as fear. According to Webster's dictionary fear is "a feeling of anxiety and agitation caused by the (perceived) presence or nearness of danger, evil, pain, etc." Yes, I definitely "perceived" that these barrels were going to smash into me and cause injury. I was literally "scared stiff." Webster's definition continues by supplying synonyms to describe fear: "timidity; dread; terror; fright; apprehension.

The fear and bodily reactions I described are the body's natural response to "fear" produced by a threatening situation. However, if our body ceases to return to normal, then we need to realize that there are two types of fear.

Two basic types of fears are:

1. Fight or flight (natural)
2. Spirits of fear (afraid, scared, worried, anxious, concerned that something bad is going to happen.)

1. Fight or Flight

There are fourteen different Hebrew words (five Greek) used in the Bible which are translated as fear.[1] The Hebrew word most often used for "fear" is *pachad* (H6343) and means sudden alarm/dread-startled. We truly are "fearfully (i.e. reverently) and wonderfully" made. God designed our bodies to respond to real dangers and return to normal stability when the danger passes. However, when our body stays in the "danger/alarm" mode for a long period of time it causes harm to our well-being emotionally, physically and spiritually. God created us to experience being startled without sustaining long-term affects or projecting fearful experiences into the future. This God-given bodily reaction is part of the flight or fight mechanism built into us for our protection.

2. Spirits of Fear

However, if we allow Satan and his spirits of fear to take this short term response mechanism and project it into the future as the basis of potential damage or present danger, he has established a demonic fear in us. The root of fear is anxiety, resulting in quaking and trembling which causes muscle stiffness. This in turn can bring on headaches and produce heart arrhythmia. Many articles from the New England Journal of Medicine tell us that the hypothalamus gland at the base of the neck is the originating point of fear, anxiety, rage, anger, stress, phobias, panic, and hostilities. The hypothalamus is the brain of the endocrine system and it is also the facilitator of the mind / body connection. For every conscious or subconscious thought that you have, there is a corresponding chemical hormone

---

[1] Strong's Numbers: Hebrew: 367, 1481, 1674, 1763, 2731, 3372, 3373, 3374, 4032, 4172, 6342, 6343, 7461, 7267 Greek: 1167, 1630, 2125, 5399, 5401. Without studying all these alternative meanings, how will you know which is intended?

neurotransmitter secretion that is supposed to bring a stability or homeostasis to your body. Yet, spiritual problems cause the secretions to be altered from "normal" levels or duration to bring "dis-ease." These are usually the result of hyper (over) or less frequently hypo (under) secretions of stabilizing hormones. This is how fear is chemically produced in our bodies.

Fear and faith are equal but opposite sides of the coin and negate or cancel each other. *Faith is the substance of things hoped for, the evidence of things not seen. (Hebrews 11:1)* Fear is the substance of things NOT hoped for, the evidence of things perceived. Both have impact upon our thoughts, actions and bodies. Sadly, we often give more credence to what we fear than who we have faith in. Both faith and fear demand to be fulfilled. It is a spiritual principle: *For as a man thinks in his heart, so is he: (Proverbs 23:7)*

We must not be ignorant of Satan's devices. (2 Cor 2:11) Fear is designed to keep us in bondage and destroy us by the principles of the spiritual kingdom. Specifically, fear's objective is often simply to remove the blessings of God, thus leading us into a circular trap that makes us disobedient to God's commands. Instead of harvesting the blessings of obedience, we incur the curse of disobedience that brings on greater fears and diseases. For example, one commandment of Jesus' was: *And as ye go, preach, saying, The kingdom of heaven is at hand. Heal the sick, cleanse the lepers, raise the dead, cast out devils: freely ye have received, freely give. (Matthew 10:7,8)*

So we step out in faith and share the gospel. In our obedience, we receive the blessings of God and his promises. Then, our righteousness is revealed as we go from faith to faith. (Fig 1)

For therein is the righteousness of God revealed from faith to faith: as it is written, The just shall live by faith. (Romans 1:17)

Command: Share the Gospel

FAITH

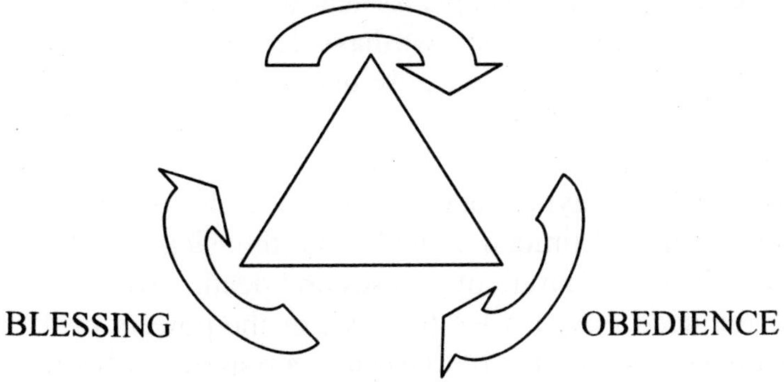

Fig 1

However, if we take on a fear of man and are so afraid that we can't share the good news of the kingdom with another, then we won't be a witness for Him. We will walk in disobedience, and receive the consequences of it. (Fig 2)

Command: Share the Gospel

FEAR OF MAN

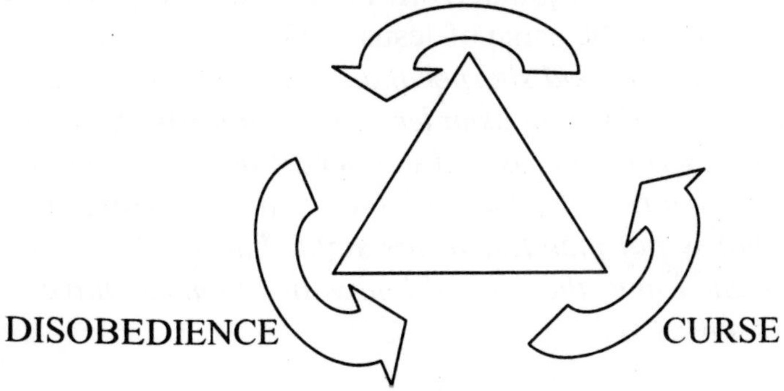

Fig 2

In other words, if faith is on the throne of our lives and we live in trust of God, then we receive His blessings because we are able to fulfill our commission as the Holy Spirit individually leads each one of us. In contrast, if we have such fear of men that we can't speak to people for fear of being rejected, shamed, or physically abused, then we have fear on the throne in that part of our lives. Do you now understand that both fear and faith demand to be fulfilled?

If someone is a hypochondriac how does he or she overcome those chains of limitation and heal the sick or cleanse the lepers? If we are afraid of corpses and death, how will we ever raise the dead? And if we fear evil or the powers of darkness, how do we cast out devils? Fear lays a trap of disobedience that steals from our faith.

The scriptures teach us that sin is:

1) a spirit being that dwells within us (Romans 7:17),
2) an attitude of disobedience (1 Samuel 15:23,24, Job 34:37) and
3) an act or thought (Matthew 5:28).

The Good News of the Gospel is that because fear is an evil spirit, it can be cast out by the Word of God, by the power of the Holy Spirit and in the name of Jesus. *For the word of God is quick, and powerful, and sharper than any two-edged sword, piercing even to the dividing asunder of* ***soul and spirit****, and of the joints and marrow, and is a discerner of the thoughts and intents of the heart. Neither is there any* ***creature*** (lit: "creation") *that is not manifest in his sight: but all things are naked and opened unto the eyes of him with whom we have to do. (Hebrews 4:12,13)*

Do you realize that fear was not initially in Adam and Eve? They were created in the image of God, and God is not fear! It was not until Adam and Eve disobeyed God's instruction not to eat of the Tree of the Knowledge of Good and Evil that they became fearful.[2] Disobedience to God's Word releases fear which compromises our immune system and leads to diseases and even death. Obedience releases God's peace and blessings of good health.

Disobedience to God, in either thought or deed, is a sin. Sin is a spirit that dwells within us. Through his disobedience, Adam allowed sin to enter into the world. His disobedience has given us a sin nature and given Satan the opening to lead us all to sin. However, our Savior, Jesus Christ, the son of obedience, made the many righteous and loosed us from the bonds of sin. *For just as through the disobedience of the one man the many were made sinners, so also through the obedience of the one man the many <u>will be made</u> righteous. (Romans 5:19 NIV)* Through Christ, we have been made free from sin[3]and given a choice to choose disobedience and sin, or obedience and righteousness.

<u>Why We Have Fear</u>

We receive fear because we disobey God and choose to allow the kingdom of darkness to have access to our life. As a result of our disobedience, God tells of the consequences: *Because I have called, and ye refused; I have stretched out my hand, and no man regarded; But ye have set at nought all my counsel, and would none of my reproof: I also will laugh at your calamity; I will mock <u>when your fear cometh</u>; When your fear cometh as*

[2] Genesis 3:9-11

[3] Romans 6:22 *But now <u>being made free from sin</u>, and become servants to God, ...*

desolation, and your destruction cometh as a whirlwind; when distress and anguish cometh upon you. Then shall they call upon me, but I will not answer; they shall seek me early, but they shall not find me: For that ***they hated knowledge, and did not choose the fear of the LORD****: They would none of my counsel: they despised all my reproof. Therefore shall they eat of the fruit of their own way, and be filled with their own devices. (Proverbs 1:24-31)*

Fear works in our thinking patterns. This passage says what we yield to will overtake us. However, this passage also concludes with a glorious promise to those who are obedient to the Word: *But whoso hearkeneth unto me shall dwell safely, and shall be quiet from fear of evil. (Proverbs 1:33)*

Job had first-hand experience in receiving the fruit of his fearful thinking. *For the thing which I greatly feared is come upon me, and that which I was afraid of is come unto me. (Job 3:25)* Both faith and fear demand a response – a response in the spiritual and in the physical. Some of those physical responses are the affects upon our bodies. Faith brings wholeness and health, and fear brings torment, sickness and disease.

Aren't you glad we have a Savior who has come to deliver us from fear so that we can worship Him? Our Lord always had a plan and promised us a way to be free from fear. *The oath which he sware to our father Abraham, that he would grant unto us, that we being delivered out of the hand of our enemies might serve him without fear, in holiness and righteousness before him, all the days of our life. (Luke 1:73-75)* He shows us, the way to make us whole. *But unto you that fear*[4] *my name shall the Sun of Righteousness arise with healing in his wings;*

[4] Hebrew: *yare'* – to revere, to frighten, to fear. This is reverential "fear", NOT demonic fear.

and ye shall go forth, and grow up as calves of the stall. (Malachi 4:2)

God is able to accomplish the object of our faith. In contrast, the demon(s) are able to execute the object of our fear and bring tremendous torment. *There is no fear in love; but perfect love casteth out fear:* ***because fear hath torment.*** *He that feareth is <u>not made perfect in love</u>. (1 John 4:18)* We need to obey. Jesus said: *If ye love me, keep my commandments. (John 14:15).* Now we know what kind of love He was talking about -- perfect love.

Some Christians think now that they are saved unto eternal life by their heart's belief and confession, they are good and wholly righteous in front of God. Many Christians ask in sincerity, just like the priests of old, "How am I disobedient?"[5] *My people are destroyed for lack of knowledge: ... (Hosea 4:6)* So we need to know God and ask Him to show us all the areas of our life wherein we lack knowledge. Every place that we walk in fear, is a place that we walk in disobedience because God says not to fear.

Example: God says: *Therefore I say unto you, Take no thought (don't fear) for your life, what ye shall eat, or what ye shall drink; nor yet for your body, what ye shall put on. Is not the life more than meat, and the body [more] than raiment? (Matthew 6:25) (also Luke 12:22, Philippians 4:6, I Peter 5:7)* We are <u>commanded</u> to have no fear of tomorrow and to trust God totally. When we take fear upon ourselves by not trusting and obeying God, then we sin. Since we know that sin is a spirit, we give an opening for that spirit to rule over us. Specifically, the spirit of fear is a ruling spirit or principality and individual fears are demons sent to bring torment and death to our life. If

[5] Malachi 1:6 …. *and ye say, Wherein have we despised thy name?*

we were perfect and totally right with God, then we should have no fear of anything. That relationship is the objective that God is working in us.

Jesus reaffirms his instructions of how to live without fear and obey his commandments in the book of Matthew; *But seek ye first the kingdom of God, and his* ***righteousness****; and all these things shall be added unto you. Take therefore no fear* (thought) *for the morrow: for the morrow shall take thought for the things of itself. Sufficient unto the day is the evil thereof. (Matthew 6:34)*

For me, the breaking of this command (*Take therefore no fear* [thought] *for the morrow.*) swung the doors wide open to the demons' assault when I was released from my job at age 53. Despite God's consistent and continual provision for our lives, I was worried and extremely fearful about taking care of my wife, meeting our needs, and the direction our lives would take without a job and a reliable paycheck. Although I had prayed for God's hand to make a way so that I could have more of Him, the idea of living by faith in all areas of my life, all the rest of my life, scared me silly. I was in great fear.

That kind of fear not only brings us under great torment, but really shows us where we stand spiritually - especially in relationship to the ministry position or "calling" God has placed upon our life.

We are to seek God's kingdom and His righteousness – first, before everything else. *But seek ye first the kingdom of God, and his righteousness;... (Matthew 6:33)*

How do we achieve righteousness? Is it simply our believing in and accepting Jesus as our Savior? No. In writings to the

believers in Rome, the scriptures say obedience to God's commands leads into righteousness and disobedience is sin unto death: *Know ye not, that to whom ye yield yourselves servants to obey, his servants ye are to whom ye obey; whether of sin unto death, or of* ***obedience unto righteousness****?*
(Romans 6:16)

At this point I want to share a spiritual principle that I experienced and my teacher, the Holy Spirit, explained to me. This insight will be logical and quickened to most, but it should also urge us toward greater vigilance. Let me tell you a little more of my experience.

At the beginning of "the dark hour of my soul," I was mindlessly driving home from an errand when I was overwhelmed by an evil spirit that made my whole body tremble inside and out. This horrible experience lasted for only minutes as I repeatedly quoted the scripture; ***For God hath not given*** **"ME"** ***the spirit of fear; but of power, and of love, and of a sound mind. (2 Timothy 1:7)*** Those few minutes seemed like they would never end. I had discerned this spirit before in the area where voodoo was practiced in Key West, Florida. However, this time I didn't need any discernment at all! I needed the big shield of Abba, my Father. I cried out for His help, but in astonishment crumbled under the overwhelming fear when His hand was withheld.

By the time I got home I had all kinds of fearful thoughts racing through my mind. When my wife got home hours later she found a writhing mass of flesh sitting in a puddle of tears. What happened? Now listen and understand.

The **spirit of fear, who is a principality**, came upon me. This powerful entity "stirred up" all the lesser demons of fear within me so that they all manifested in my body, mind and emotions. These underling spirits of fear are the specific fears like fear of man, fear of pain, fear of tomorrow, fear of death, etc. God has given us authority to expel these fears with the power of the Holy Spirit in the name of Jesus. Before we can do that, we need to know that they are there, and to walk in faith and knowledge under Holy Spirit led obedience to the Word of God.

This is the same spiritual principle that we observe when the Holy Spirit is given control of our life and infills and "anoints" us with His Spirit. When we are empowered, do not the spirits of God manifest? I am often teaching or speaking under the power of the Holy Spirit and say things that are even a mystery to me. How? I do so because one of the Spirits of God is manifesting in me. What are the Spirits of God? According to Isaiah 11:2; *And the **spirit** of the LORD shall rest upon him, the **spirit** of wisdom and understanding, the **spirit** of counsel and might, the **spirit** of knowledge and of the fear[6] of the LORD;*

In the example given, we can understand that the Spirits' of God are speaking through the teacher by the empowering Holy Spirit. The Spirit of Wisdom, Understanding and Knowledge will often manifest in an anointed teacher. Similarly, when the demons flee while ministering deliverance under the power of the Holy Spirit, we can understand that the Spirit of Might is coming forth through the minister.

The critical thing we must discern is who rules over our life to manifest his spirits? Does the Holy Spirit "stir up" the spirits of God that Jesus possessed without measure as He comes upon

---

[6] Hebrew: *yare'* – to revere, to frighten, to fear. This is reverential "fear", NOT demonic fear.

us? Or does a demonic principality, like the spirit of fear, "stir up" his subordinate fears whom we have allowed to reign in us for lack of knowledge, obedience and faith in God?

In talking about the tongue, James asks *Doth a fountain send forth at the same place sweet water and bitter? (James 3:11)* And he also says: *Out of the same mouth proceedeth blessing and cursing. My brethren, these things ought not so to be. (James 3:10)* He doesn't say that it **isn't so**, but rather that **it shouldn't be so** that we have evil and good coming out of our heart-wells. Our charge is to become Christ-like and expel all the evil so that the enemy has nothing in us to "hook" or take us into sin. We are to be holy as He is holy because 1 Peter 1:16 commands: *...Be ye holy; for I am holy.*

What God Thinks of Fear

*But the **fearful**, and unbelieving, and the abominable, and murderers, and whoremongers, and sorcerers, and idolaters, and all liars, shall have their part in the lake which burneth with fire and brimstone: which is the second death.*
(Revelation 21:8) The Greek word "fearful" in this passage connotes "faithless" and only appears twice in the Bible. This scripture does not mean that if we succumb to a spirit of fear that we are destined for hell. This is a state of practicing fear because we haven't walked in faith.

The antidote to fear is to trust and obey God. The acceptance of fear says that fear is more powerful than God. However, the Word says: *Every word of God is pure: he is a shield unto them that put their trust in him. (Proverbs 30:5)* Also, Isaiah 26:3 says, *Thou wilt keep him in perfect peace, whose mind is stayed on thee: because he trusteth in thee.*

There is an exchange that must happen for health and healing for our life. Jesus must be part of our life. Jesus must not only be part of it, but truly the Lord of our life. Neither we ourselves, nor the domination of the devil's thoughts can be the ruler of our life. We must exchange our fears for trust in God. We must truly believe Him when He says, *Lo, I am with you always even unto the end of the world. (Matthew 28:20) Yea, though I walk through the valley of the shadow of death, I will fear no evil: for* ***thou art with me****; thy rod and thy staff they comfort me. (Psalms 23:4)*

We can be in faith, with fear raging inside also. What does the Bible say we should do when we have done all we know and have mounted up with all the faith we can summon? *For we wrestle not against flesh and blood, but against principalities, against powers, against the rulers of the darkness of this world, against spiritual wickedness in high places. Wherefore take unto you the whole armour of God, that ye may be able to withstand in the evil day, and* ***having done all, to stand.*** *(Ephesians 6:12,13)*

One of my daughters has been plagued with neck, shoulder, lower back, leg, hip and ankle pain initially caused by damage sustained from sports and childbirth. She believed that she had been directed by the Holy Spirit to seek some chiropractic help - but not to rely upon it. Just before coming home this past holiday season, she felt the Lord tell her to cancel her chiropractor's appointment. So she did. Then, just as soon as she did, she began to worry whether or not she would feel all right during her visit. When she reconsidered keeping the appointment, she became fearful (as a result of past experience) that he might not adjust her properly and leave her in worse shape than she was.

After sharing this with me, I was able to show her that she was not only having her faith tested, but that the spirits of fear were trying to put her in bondage. Let's examine this step by step because it will demonstrate some more principles of the spiritual kingdom:

1. Upon stepping out in faith (believing the Word to cancel the appointment), **fears will try to launch a counter attack in order to thwart or nullify your faith.**

2. **Fear will build upon fear.** Fear will build upon fear to the extent we will allow it. It is the same principle that God tells us about gaining knowledge of His Word. We are to build precept upon precept. Similarly, the enemy has a counterfeit kingdom principle to build fear upon fear.

    a. First fear - questioning if she would be all right

    b. Second fear - doubting if the adjustment would work

    c. Third fear - questioning <u>if it was the word of God</u> she received as she stepped out in faith to cancel the doctor's appointment in the first place.

3. **Increasing fears will try to lay a seemingly irresolvable trap**. She feared to go without adjustment. However, if she did go, she feared being worse off. Her dilemma was to go or not to go. If we are unable to resolve the issue logically, the anxiety usually becomes greater and greater until a decision is made and its consequences accepted. (Accepting responsibility for our decisions is a big issue also. This issue will be discussed in chapter 9.)

While this type of merry-go-round trap can be a disaster waiting to eat us alive, it places us in an opportune position for our faith to be strengthened. We need to understand this clearly: There is no resolution to the problem, only potential consequences. The only solution is to rise up in the armor of our faith **and stand** upon our trust and faith in God's Word. As a matter of fact the only "logical" solution is to stand upon the preceding (first) word, because while we may be a little unsure of its origin, we can be certain of the origin of the following "words" or thoughts because they bring fear.

It is good to discuss these things with someone so that we can get our thoughts out on the table and exposed to the light. However, there has to be an environment of love so that the light of the truth doesn't bring condemnation or rejection upon ourselves. (Don't share with someone who is unloving toward us and whose counsel we don't trust. In other words, don't give the devil further opportunity to slam us.)

Don't let a fear of exposure, embarrassment or shame (which is pride) set a never ending, merry-go-round trap. For the sake of our very life, we must get fears out to be viewed in the light of the truth – God's Word. We often don't formalize our thoughts enough to "see" them when we don't express them audibly. Unfortunately, we are so easily deceived when it comes to our own "stuff."

I'd like to praise God and his faithfulness. Upon my daughter's arrival my wife and I prayed for her. Three days later the Lord did His own adjustment and aligned her hips perfectly level. This is a position they have not been in for several years. God also took away great back discomfort and numbness in her leg. It was a joyous confirmation of how God leads and honors our faith in His Word. We have to allow God's light to dispel the darkness. The light of the Word mixed with faith will overcome fear. The good news of the gospel is:

- Fear is not greater than God.
- Fear is not greater than the Word of God.
- Fear is not greater than faith.

Fear reminds us of our shortcomings and projects them into the future – a bad future. It will try to get us to settle for second best. For the believer this is especially true concerning our destiny and the will of God for our life. *And be not conformed to this world: but be ye transformed by the renewing of your mind, that ye may prove what is that good, and acceptable, and perfect, will of God. (Romans 12:2)* We must not settle for the "good" will of God for our life because fear holds us back from greater faith and trust in Him and the Word.

We must make a decision that we, and all that we have, are the Lord's. Whether we live or die, we are the Lord's. If we live and do great works for the Lord, then hallelujah for the glory brought to the throne. But, what happens if we die? We'll go to heaven and be with the Lord always. *..lo, I am with you alway, even unto the end of the world. Amen. (Matthew 28:20)* This is not to suggest that death is a good desire, but rather, we are not to fear death. We are to be as the apostle when he says: *For whether we live, we live unto the Lord; and whether we die, we die unto the Lord: whether we live therefore, or die, we are the Lord's. (Romans 14:8)*

Chapter 1
Summary

1. Fears unrelated to present physical danger are spirits.

2. Fears are the opposites and the enemies of faith. God's way is faith.

3. Before their original sin, Adam and Eve did not have fears.

4. Fears have come into our lives because we have ignored or not heard the Word of God. Fears gain entry through our generations and our acts of disobedience to kingdom principles and God's laws.

5. Walking in righteousness is a walk of obedience to God.

6. The Lord commands us not to be fearful.

7. Fear generates more fears.

8. Multiple fears lay seemingly irresolvable traps.

Chapter Two

The Faces of Fear

Three Most Common fears

The three fears most common to mankind are:

1. Fear of man,
2. Fear of evil, and
3. Fear of death.

We must get our hearts in line to fight these fears if we are going to become the man/woman of God we're destined to be. We put too much emphasis on how we feel. Have you ever considered that how we "feel" might not be who we are at all? Many voices of thought come at us: [7]

- God by the Holy Spirit
- Your own spirit and intellect
- Satan's kingdom

Who do our thoughts line up with? We must begin: *Casting down imaginations, and every high thing that exalteth itself against the knowledge of God, and bringing into captivity every thought to the obedience of Christ;... (2 Cor 10:5)* We can't keep listening to lies and be all that God has called us to be.

[7] Someone else's words can be echoed by any of the three.

We have to listen to, and believe in, God's Word – the antidote to fears.

1. Fear of Man

Some examples of antidotes to one of our biggest fears – the fear of man, are:

The LORD is on my side; I will not fear: what can man do unto me? (Psa 118:6)

In God I will praise his word, in God I have put my trust; I will not fear what flesh can do unto me. (Psa 56:4)

Fear of man will keep you from believing and obeying God. In the book of I Samuel we read the story about Israel's first king. King Saul was a "goodly" man blessed and anointed by God to be King over Israel (I Samuel 9:17). However, his fear of man caused him to disobey God and sin by offering animal sacrifice when he was not a Levite priest.[8] His disobedience and fear of man, or what we sometimes label a man pleasing spirit, brought him torment from the evil spirit "sent by God." It cost him God's anointing, kingship over Israel and his very life.

Fear of Man spirits include:

- fear of man (all man-pleasing spirits)
- rejection
- failure
- abandonment

I believe that in the United States the fear of man became a stronger and a more dominant spirit as our culture transitioned from an agricultural based society through industrialization and

[8] By God's commission, only a Levite priest could slay the sacrifice.

now to a financial/technical one. When the farmer was solely responsible for his own provision most interpersonal relationships were based on mutual cooperation, interests and respect. Today, in our hierarchal workplaces, competition exists among co-workers and distrust and fear reigns in worker/management relationships because of conflicting goals. The worker is trying to make a living and progress along a career path whereas upper management is demonstrating less and less loyalty toward their workers by yielding to the pressures of short-range profit goals.

The advertising business in which I worked for more than thirty years was on the forefront of this move. When I began in the business, it was understood that job security was nonexistent because the agency's very existence depended upon the continuing business of the major clients. While individuals often moved from agency to agency in order to get ahead, there was a degree of "family" and job security within an agency. However, then employee-owned agencies were bought out by larger public agencies, which were in turn bought out by conglomerates, etc. As a result of these mergers and buy-outs, the only hope for job security was in the achievement of profit goals. If they could not be achieved, then personnel were basically the only significant cost item that could be cut to achieve bottom line results. Thus, instead of employees having genuine respect for management because they were jointly trying to assure the workers' jobs, that "respect" turned to fear.

In my "walk-out" from the clutches of many fears, I was surprised when the Holy Spirit revealed that the fear of man had been a significant factor in my life. I had worked my way up through the ranks until I was a Managing Partner and member of the Board of Directors. Although I never thought that I feared men, I had, in fact, looked to many other people for approval and recognition. I was constantly trying to please others and appear morally correct, but not with the right motives. Instead of living and "doing works" out of the love of God, I lived in the fear of abandonment and rejection by men (and women) in all areas of my life. Thus, if rejection by man was a high possibility, then without compromising my testimony, I made choices and unknowingly held beliefs that were based upon the criteria of man, rather than upon God's Word.

For example, up until the last decade of my working career, I remember being very hesitant to give testimony of my faith in Jesus Christ around those who were obviously hostile to the gospel or me. I would fall into the trap of rationalization that I shouldn't "cast my pearls before swine," and walked merrily along in the enemy's deception that I didn't fear man. In truth, I was fearful that my testimony would cause ridicule and potentially jeopardize my relationship with an individual who could have an impact upon my well-being.

Whether in the business world or at home, interpersonal relationships that are motivated by other fears such as the fear of rejection, disapproval, not being loved, loneliness, etc., are a prime indicator that we have a fear of man hiding behind our own rationalization. Until we can trust and look only to the Lord for our love and well-being, we will be battling the fear of man that permeates our society.

Also, as we give into the fear of man we are often wounded because we are looking to others for something they might not even know that you are expecting them to provide. These woundings can then lead to bitterness which Paul calls a gall or poison within us. *For I perceive that thou art in the gall of bitterness, and in the bond of iniquity. (Acts 8:23)*

Bitterness is a powerful holding spirit that gives an opening to other evil spirits. Paul calls it a "bond" of iniquity. In other words, bitterness can keep us held to sin. As we will see in a moment, bitterness has the same holding power to sin as the fear of death.

2. Fear of Evil

Fear of Evil is another one of the major fears we have to defeat in our lives in order that we are able to carry out Jesus' commission to heal the sick and set the captives free.

This fear says:

- Satan is bigger than God and God's promises
- Evil can defeat God
- Bad things are going to happen to you, and
- That you need to fantasize/consider destruction in order to protect yourself.

Can you see the trap being set with fantasizing? Although chapter 3 will talk about the dangers of fantasizing, let me briefly develop this idea here, because we have to begin discerning the traps that our enemy sets for us.

- **God says** that we are to take no thought of tomorrow. (Matthew 6:34)
- The **fear of evil says** fantasize about tomorrow's potential destruction to protect ourselves.
- **God says** that our obedience to His Word will bring His protection and our disobedience will bring fear. (Proverbs 1:24-32)

If we've allowed ourselves to fantasize destruction, we are already in sin through disobedience to God's Word. Disobedience invites fear. Thus, a tendency to fantasize destruction means the fear of evil is ruling one's thoughts. The only way out of the trap is repentance and resistance to this spirit's "voice."

Some examples of the fear of evil include:

- obsessive concern over exposure to chemicals or agents that we consider harmful i.e. toxins, concentrated acids, carcinogens, etc.
- worrying about negative affects from people who do not consider our needs
- fear of Satan and his kingdom
- fear of personal assault from evil doers.

We have to be men and women of faith, not only when the fear and bodily reactions are gone from the fears we carry today, but also when we find ourselves in trials that come our way in the future. We must learn to trust God with an increasing faith/belief in His Word and daily salvation for our lives.

<u>God commands us not to fear evil.</u>
*And I said unto you, I am the LORD your God; **fear not the gods** of the Amorites, in whose land ye dwell: but ye have not obeyed my voice. (Judges 6:10)* People have great fear of Satanism, voodoo, etc. Taking in <u>fear is a sin</u>.

Encouraging words in the scriptures are sometimes a command as well: *Thou shalt not be afraid for the terror by night (Night terror, dreams and visions); nor for the arrow that flieth by day (fear of accusation slander); Nor for the pestilence that walketh in darkness; nor for the destruction that wasteth at noonday. (Psalms 91:5,6)*

Let not your heart be troubled, neither let it be afraid. (John 14:27)

Say ye not, a confederacy, to all them to whom this people shall say, a confederacy; neither fear ye their fear, nor be afraid. (Isaiah 8:12)

Wherefore take unto you the whole armour of God, that ye may be able to withstand in the evil day, and ***having done all, to stand****. (Eph 6:13)*

The issue we have to resolve is, "Does God protect and walk us through evil or not?" *Yea, though I walk through the valley of the* ***shadow of death****, I will fear no evil: for thou art with me; thy rod and thy staff they comfort me. (Psa 23:4)* Do we really believe in the Word and trust the Lord? If we don't, and we fear evil or Satan and his kingdom, we will probably also have, or be open to acquire a spirit that is called fear of death.

3. Fear of Death

Fear of Death is insidious and manifests in our thinking in many different and subtle ways. It is not just the fear of dying in the flesh. It manifests itself in fear of losing God, fear of losing our salvation, fear of losing our mental faculties, fear of losing our identity, fear of illness, fear of incapacitation and on and on. *And deliver them who through fear of death were all their lifetime* ***subject to bondage****. (Hebrews 2:15)*

By knowing this Word of God, we can understand how this spirit of fear is a powerful "gatekeeper" of the soul. As a "gatekeeper" he is one who, because he has so many other spirits under his domain, can prevent or allow many spirits of fear in or out of his dwelling. **The expulsion of this fear is**

key to freeing you from many other spirits of fear. But, the good news is that Jesus overcame death and rose to life again so that in Him, we might have victory over death. Now we don't have to fear death because he; *hath raised us up together, and made us sit together in heavenly places in Christ Jesus: (Ephesians 2:6)* **Hallelujah!**

Jesus said: *For whosoever will save his life* (fear of death) *shall lose it* (physically and by worrying it away)*; but whosoever shall lose his life for my sake and the gospel's, the same shall save it. (Mark 8:35)*

All three of these major fears are subtly crushing Christians' faith every day. When I was so messed up in the darkest hours of God's disciplining, I had to use Celexia, a Prozac type anti-depressant. I had resisted taking an anti-depressant for more than six months, but finally took the doctor's recommendation in order to function at all. I felt very guilty and defeated in using the drug because I previously had walked in great faith (and results) for God's supernatural healing.

I now realize that all these types of drugs are really a substitute for the Holy Spirit and faith in God. Yet, I believe God was doing more than delivering me from fear by allowing me to become so desperate that I would look only to Him and never again be tempted to judge another. So as you fight your way to freedom, remember not to wallow in self condemnation because God is accomplishing much more in you than simply ridding you of your fears.

> *The sacrifices of God are a broken spirit: a broken and a contrite heart, O God, thou wilt not despise. (Psalms 51:17*

Wisdom vs. Fear

Using wisdom does not necessarily mean we are in fear. When we take provision to avoid evil, we don't have to receive fear. If we are shocked by a frayed electric wire, is it wisdom or fear to replace worn wires? However, if we let that experience (i.e. electric shock) make us afraid to plug in a lamp, then we have received a fear of electricity. That's why we must face our fears and defeat them. If we don't, they will rule our lives just as sure as one who has a fear embedded into their soul so strongly that it becomes a phobia.

We simply must believe and obey God's Word to us. Do you know that we step on snakes and scorpions when we bring our thoughts into captivity?[9] And by doing so, the enemy can not inflict his consequences because we have obeyed Jesus' commission and not sinned against God. If we don't bring our thoughts into captive alignment with His Word, then we must recognize that we are in rebellion to God's commandment.

Rebellion is a form of witchcraft, and idolatry, because we have declared our opposition to God. We have given ourselves and thoughts of intellect, or the devil's input, preeminence over God's commandments. We have made ourselves gods and not the creation that God formed. We need to cultivate our discernment between good and evil and identify the origin of our thoughts. Are they from God, the enemy or self?

[9] Luke 10:19 *Behold, I give unto you power to tread on serpents and scorpions, and over all the power of the enemy: and nothing shall by any means hurt you.*

You will recall from the beginning of this study - for every conscious or subconscious thought that we have, there is a corresponding chemical hormone neurotransmitter secretion that is supposed to bring a stability or homeostasis to our body. Because of spiritual problems those secretions can be altered from "normal" levels or duration to inhibit our immune system from normal functioning. This inability to balance our bodily functions and fight off infections brings disease. Generally the secretions from the hypothalamus tend to be excessive.

When we are continually shadow-boxing against these fears and becoming more and more stressed, we are constantly giving our body excessive hormonal secretions until we become exhausted. This is the last stage of the body's malfunction. We become repeatedly exhausted from conscious and subconscious fears that trigger a system that was designed for homeostasis or stability of our body. I believe many Christians are only treating the symptoms by saturating their bodies with mega doses of vitamins and health food supplements. We must begin to recognize that the root problem is spiritual and not physical.

Two Characteristics of Fear

1. Fear is **contagious**: Both faith and fear exist and manifest in the spiritual and in the physical dimension. Not only do they both demand a response, they both can be contagious. *Then the officers shall add, "Is any man afraid or fainthearted? Let him go home so that his brothers will not become disheartened too." (Deuteronomy 20:8 NIV)*

2. Fear can be a **self-fulfilling** prophecy: *For the thing which I greatly feared is come upon me, and that which*

> *I was afraid of is come unto me. (Job 3:25)*
>
> *I also will choose their delusions, and will bring their fears upon them; because when I called, none did answer; when I spake, they did not hear: but they did evil before mine eyes, and chose that in which I delighted not. (Isaiah 66:4)*

There is an element in fear that brings death and not life: *There is no fear in love; but perfect love casteth out fear:* ***because fear hath torment****. He that feareth is not made perfect in love. (1 John 4:18)*

Chapter 2
<u>Summary</u>

1. Fear can rob us of our anointing and destiny in Christ.
2. Fear of death is the "glue" or bonding agent in the Spirit of Fear's domain.
3. Wisdom is not fear.
4. Fears are contagious.
5. Fears can become self-fulfilling.

Chapter Three

Phobias

I once got in a scuffle with an obese, older boy when I was in my early grade school years. Instead of pounding me with his fists, the youngster pushed me down to the ground and jumped on top of me. Before long, I was gasping for breath as his weight crushed it out of me. I was desperate to the point of panic. Although I didn't recall this situation until years later, from that day forth I would nearly panic if I was restrained or weighty things were placed upon me. When I reached high school I tried out for wrestling in order to stay in shape between the football and baseball seasons. Although the coach said I was a "natural," my participation was short-lived because I hated the sport. Specifically, I <u>really</u> disliked being restrained and covered by an opponent.

Shortly thereafter I was introduced to scuba diving. In the preliminary shallow water dives, I loved the freedom and the wide open expanse of this colorful new world. However, the first time we dove in deeper waters I began to gasp for air in panic! I didn't think about why, I didn't reason my way out of it, I just shot for the surface (a very bad move) because I was suffocating – or so I "thought!" The weight of the water pressure upon my body made me feel trapped. After that experience I could hardly put my head beneath the water's surface without discomfort. Then, finally I would become uneasy, my throat would tighten and I would breathe faster even when I came near the water's edge. This irrational association lasted for several months until I faced my fear.

Was my panic of being near water a phobia? Webster's dictionary defines a phobia as, "an irrational, excessive, and persistent fear of some particular thing or situation." Yes, my reaction was a textbook phobic response.

Unlike my phobia, which was caused by associated experiences, the experts reports that many phobias appear to be associated with a family history of fear and anxiety disorders. A generational curse is often biological in nature due to a defective gene affecting the vital functions and process of the individual. This gene is a part of the physiological make-up (in contrast to the soul or spirit) of the individual. The controlling physiological process and response mechanisms reside along with the soul, within the brain. (In contrast, the spirit of man and the Holy Spirit resides in the vicinity of the belly.) If these response mechanisms have been altered from their natural homeostasis by fear, then they interfere with your natural biological processes. Thus, a phobia may sometimes be associated with a physiological defect that affects our soul.

It is like a computer virus that interferes with the process of association and computation. In a phobic response, the body generally produces a high state of anxiety and fear to situations or objects that in of themselves shouldn't be threatening. For example: A normal person will not feel threatened with being crushed or trapped in a six foot by six foot room. However, a person with claustrophobia will be fighting panic in an elevator of that size.

Because phobias are often associated with a family history of fear and anxiety disorders, the anxiety produced by a phobic response is often a fearful reaction to the potential emergence of unconscious drives. It is a reaction that is expressed in excessive activity of the autonomic (automatic) nervous system. Anxiety begins in thought, but expresses itself physiologically through the nervous system. Not only does the nervous system come into play, but so also does the endocrine system (hormone-producing glands) which produces chemicals manufactured by your hypothalamus gland. So you get a "double whammy."

"However, further psychological (soul) mechanisms (mindsets, units of memory, emotions, programming of thoughts,) are reinforced by evil spirits. That's why even when we are delivered from evil spirits we have to have our mind renewed and replace the evil thoughts. <u>We have to face our fears</u>."

Phobias' psychological manifestations are **<u>projections</u> and <u>displacement</u>** (avoidance). These manifestations in and of themselves can become a way of thinking and life. If carried to the extreme of association they can result in environmental allergies. One might say, "How can I avoid (displace) this thing that will hurt me (projection)? I will avoid it by……" At this stage the person has become one with the fear and much of their thought life is centered on avoidance (displacement). As they begin to fear one thing and their immune system becomes compromised, then something else that is associated with the first object of fear can affect them also (example on next page).

This associated item can be purely irrational, but often is similar in some sensory (shape, smell, touch, size, etc.) manner. If your immune system is further compromised by this additional fear, it can be projected to another object, then another and another until you have full blown Multiple Chemical Sensitivities/ Environmental Illness (MCS/EI).

Three stages of Phobic response

1. At stage one, fear/anxiety have an object (an external situation or object) which can then progress to an association or representation of the thing. Simplified example: A dog bites a person. Then at the stage of association, all living animals may provoke fear. It happens with smells and sounds as well as sight objects.

2. At stage two, fear/anxiety is generally subconscious. Continuing with our example of the dog-bitten person: toy stuffed dogs (or even animals) create anxiety, but they can't understand why. Sometimes the individual doesn't even know what is causing the anxiety. They might know the fear comes while in the child's room and begin associating children with their fear.

3. At stage three, fear/anxiety causes exhaustion. The repeated boosted infusion of hormones in the bloodstream can lead to the depletion of needed vitamins, and specifically potassium. A long-term decrease in potassium levels cause fatigue.

The choice of the phobic symbol is often determined by a chance exposure to the object at a time when the anxiety over a threatening inner impulse first appeared. In other words the phobic object becomes a conditioned stimulus. And the phobic neurosis is a learned response. The nearer the person comes to the phobic object the greater the anxiety and fear mounts. Then the individual tries to avoid the stimulus, inhibiting his daily life and capacity to function normally.

<u>Symptoms and signs:</u>
Frequently, the very thought of the phobic object is sufficient to produce anxiety. The object can be anything: smells, objects, animals, mold, and even other people, such as the pastor. Some individuals associate intense people with victimization. Thus, pastor phobia is real because some ministers of the Word are intense. We need to separate ourselves and others from our fears. If we are unable to do so, then we and our minister have a major obstacle to conquer before we can deal with the root cause and be delivered. If we are full of rejection, we'll think the one ministering is mad at us. Then the trap will stay shut unless we break it open with the **believed Word of God.**

<u>Panic and Panic Attacks:</u>
"Panic is fear accelerated though a mixture of the involuntary nervous system and the endocrine system." The seat of all panic attacks is the hypothalamus gland that is responding to a spiritual problem – real or imagined. When the fear is accelerated the bloodstream is filled with a hormone ACTH, your heart races, breath is short, you can't think, blood is restricted and sometimes you'll faint.

<u>Panic attacks without any stressor present are direct evidence of an evil spirit.</u> It is something invisible that is controlling you… without any stimulus. There is a spirit of panic as well as fear.

<u>The Enemy Within</u>

Jesus said, *For from within, out of the heart of men, proceed evil thoughts, adulteries, fornications, murders, thefts, covetousness, wickedness, deceit, lasciviousness, an evil eye, blasphemy, pride, foolishness: All these evils come from within, and defile the man. (Mark 7:22,23)*

Some Christians believe that this teaching doesn't apply to them because they have been taught that a Christian can not have a demon within them, influencing their actions. While I generally tend to address this controversy frankly and directly, I would first like to relate a story recently told to me by a beloved man of God who oversees hundreds of churches in Central and West Africa, Apostle Emmanuel Jibuike of Logos, Nigeria.

The Story:

There was a young girl in one of his assemblies who grew up in a Christian family, made a profession of faith, was baptized in water and by the Holy Spirit, had a gift for evangelism, and was very active in the church. By all outward appearances and by the discernment of the Holy Spirit through others, she was a true disciple of Jesus Christ. She had always acted very normal and on fire for the Lord. However, the night before her wedding she disappeared without taking any extra clothing or money. Three days later she turned up in a village more than a hundred miles away. She could not remember anything about her journey. However, it was apparent that she had walked the hundred plus miles through the bush as evidenced by her torn clothing and scratched arms and legs. When she was attended to, she spoke in a deep-toned man's voice repeatedly declaring that, "He (meaning the groom to be) couldn't have her. She is mine. She belongs to me." When the ministering pastors demanded that the evil spirits leave her in the name of Jesus Christ, she shook profusely and fell unconscious as the spirit(s) departed.

Although the ministering pastors couldn't determine how the demon had an opening to enter the girl, it had apparently been with her for a long time. She returned home to marry the young man and is reported to be living a good life, raising a family, and regularly attending church.

To our civilized Western society this story may seem extreme. As a result, many Christians choose to ignore many similar testimonies that are echoed throughout the world. In my ministry, here in the United States, I have personally discerned and witnessed the release of many vocal demonic spirits coming out of professing believers. This is why I believe that the teaching that a Christian can't have a demon is a lie from the pit of hell to keep God's people captive to Satan's control and kingdom. Given over to our own lack of knowledge, Satan's kingdom can become so influential in a Christian's life that it becomes difficult to separate the individual from the spirits that are talking through them.

Let's consider this controversy from a scriptural perspective.

After more than 30 years of walking the way that Jesus instructed the ecclesia (i.e. church/called out ones), Paul, <u>a redeemed, born again apostle of God</u> understood the problem, the enemy and **where he dwelt**: *For that which I do I allow not: for what I would, that do I not; but what I hate, that do I. If then I do that which I would not, I consent unto the law that it is good. Now then it is no more I that do it, but* ***sin that dwelleth in me.*** *For I know that in me (that is, in my flesh,) dwelleth no good thing: for to will is present with me; but how to perform that which is good I find not. For the good that I would I do not: but the evil which I would not, that I do. Now if I do that I would not, it is no more I that do it, but* ***sin that dwelleth*** *in me.*

I find then a law (a proclamation or principle), that, when I would do good, evil is present with me. (Satan has his law of mind/body "physics" operating and regulating us from within us.) *For I delight in the law of God after the inward man*: (We have to allow the Holy Spirit to write the laws i.e. the regulation and regulators of our body – in our hearts.[10]) *But I see another law in my members, warring against the law of my mind, and bringing me into captivity to the law of sin which is in my members. O wretched man that I am! who shall deliver me from the body of this death? I thank God through Jesus Christ our Lord. So then with the mind I myself serve the law of God; but with the flesh the law of sin. (Romans 7:15-25)*

Where did we get this nature? Did we get this from God?

No!!

For God hath not given us the spirit of fear; but of power* (God the Holy Spirit), *and of love* (God the Father), *and of a sound mind* (God the Word –Jesus). *- 2 Timothy 1:7

The antidote to fear is obedience to God's instructions. This is a work of the Holy Spirit because only He can empower and enable us to be obedient to God's instructions. This walk must come out of a heart of trusting and loving God and His Word. If we are only obedient to God's commands by knowledge, we are in jeopardy of bondage to the laws. However, if we want to obey God's commands because we love him, then we are a "free man" and joyful in the performance of His instructions. When fear is present it tries to dominate us and push aside our

---

[10] Isiah 51:7 *Hearken unto me, ye that know righteousness, the people* ***in whose heart is my law****; fear ye not the reproach of men, neither be ye afraid of their revilings.*

faith from the Holy Spirit. Fear is NOT, "just the way we are," or our personality! It is a spirit that is controlling us.

Generational Curses

We must understand that "just the way we are" is not only the result of our disobedience, but our ancestors' disobedience as well. Generational traits go far beyond genetic heritage, especially when referring to our personalities. Speaking through Moses, God says, *If thou wilt not observe to do all the words of this law that are written in this book, that thou mayest fear this glorious and fearful name, THE LORD THY GOD; Then the LORD will make thy plagues wonderful, and the plagues of thy seed, even great plagues, and of long continuance, and sore sicknesses, and of long continuance. (Deu 28:58, 59)* In the understanding of what we now know about sin, fear, and spirits, what is this saying? Isn't this saying that since we know that disobedience to God's commands are sin, and fear is the plague of sin, then we inherit the plagues (fears) of our ancestors?

While we quote the first part of the next verse, we prefer to omit the rest of the verse because it says our sin would affect our children and grandchildren. *My people are destroyed for lack of knowledge: because thou hast rejected knowledge, I will also reject thee, that thou shalt be no priest to me: seeing thou hast forgotten the law of thy God, I will also forget thy children. (Hosea 4:6)*

As I testified earlier, all types of fears overwhelmed me when they were "stirred up" during my time of greatest trauma. Sometimes I had no knowledge that I was fearful of a specific thing until the Lord graciously revealed what I feared. While they may have come from my disobedience to His Word, they didn't all come from my specific experience of embracing that particular fear. This is the same phenomenon to which I referred when speaking about phobias and their subconscious associations.

For example, my father suffered a nervous breakdown while yet in his thirties. I never consciously feared having a nervous breakdown because I was very self sufficient and blessed with good thinking abilities. Yet, when all my fears began to manifest and my thinking became so clouded that I could barely remember anything other than yesterday's torment, I became extremely fearful of going insane. It was a hidden fear received from my father who had to care for his father (my grandfather) in his old-age dementia.

God is so merciful and gracious to His children. He does not want us to succumb to the wiles of the enemy. He will give us the knowledge and the way, through Jesus Christ, to overcome every fear of the enemy. However, we have a responsibility to ourselves and to our children. We absolutely must break these curses or "plagues" by asking God's forgiveness and renouncing the sins of our ancestors as well as ourselves.[11]

As discussed on page 11, Adam and Eve were not created with the demonic fears we have been talking about. They were created in the image of God, and God is not fear! God is the God of peace. Adam's disobedience to God's commandments brought fear into him.[12] Even today, disobedience to God's Word is sin and it releases fear into our lives. However, obedience brings the peace of God. *Those things, which ye*

[11] See Chapter 9 – Overcoming Fear
[12] Genesis 3:9-11

---

have both learned, and received, and heard, and seen in me, do: and ***the God of peace*** *shall be with you. (Philippians 4:9)*

Relationship with God

Our relationship with God is our protection: *He that dwelleth in the secret place of the most High shall abide under the shadow of the Almighty. I will say of the LORD, He is my refuge and my fortress: my God; in him will I trust. Surely he shall deliver thee from the snare of the fowler, and from the noisome pestilence. He shall cover thee with his feathers, and under his wings shalt thou trust:* ***his truth*** **(WORD)** ***shall be thy shield and buckler.***[13] *Thou shalt not be afraid* (FEAR) *for the terror by night; nor for the arrow that flieth by day; Nor for the pestilence* (FEAR OF DISEASE) *that walketh in darkness*; nor for the destruction (FEAR OF DESTRUCTION/LOSING YOUR LIFE) *that wasteth at noonday. (Psa 91:1-6)* Did you know that disobedience (sin) separates us from God and keeps us from dwelling in the "secret place of the most High?"

It is only through our sanctification that we can dwell in that protected place. We will discuss this coveted positioning more thoroughly in Chapter 5.

---

[13] Ephesians 6

Chapter 3
Summary

1. A phobia is an irrational, excessive and consistent fear projection, often to specific objects or situations.

2. Phobias' psychological manifestations are **projections** (to objects or situations) and **displacement** (avoidance).

3. Non-generational phobias generally begin in the consciousness, become subconscious and can eventually lead to exhaustion.

4. The enemy, fear can dwell within us.

5. Our relationship with God is our protection from all fears.

Chapter Four

Antidotes

What is the antidote for fear? It is faith in God's Word.

And where does faith come from? Faith comes from hearing. Hearing what? Faith comes from hearing the Word of God. (*So then faith cometh by hearing, and hearing by the word of God. (Romans 10:17)* Faith comes when the Holy Spirit speaks the Word into our spirits. Faith is a fruit of the Holy Spirit.[14] So when fear comes upon us where is the medicine cabinet? The Word of God is the medicine cabinet the Holy Spirit opens for us. *For unto us was the gospel preached, as well as unto them: but the word preached did not profit them, not being mixed with faith in them that heard it. For we which have believed do enter into rest.... (Hebrews 4:2, 3)* Are you in rest today?

In order to gain knowledge, we have to know our position in Him by and through the Word of God. We need to be, *sanctified by the washing of water by the Word.* (Ephesians 5:26) *Every word of God is pure: he is a shield unto them that put their trust in him. (Proverbs 30:5)* Remember: *All scripture is given by inspiration of God, and is profitable for doctrine, for reproof, for correction, for instruction in righteousness: That the man of God may be perfect, thoroughly furnished unto all good works. (2 Tim 3:16, 17)*

---

[14] Galatians 5:22 *But the fruit of the Spirit is love, joy, peace, longsuffering, gentleness, goodness,* ***faith***,..

My son, attend to my words; incline thine ear unto my sayings. Let them not depart from thine eyes; keep them in the midst of thine heart. For they are life unto those that find them, and ***health to all their flesh.*** *(Prov 4:20-22)*

Let us review Proverbs 1:24 again. We studied this in the first chapter to understand why we get in fear. But this time let's read a little further for the antidote we've been talking about. *Because I have called, and ye refused; I have stretched out my hand, and no man regarded; But ye have set at nought all my counsel, and would none of my reproof: I also will laugh at your calamity; I will mock when your fear cometh; When your fear cometh as desolation, and your destruction cometh as a whirlwind; when distress and anguish cometh upon you. Then shall they call upon me, but I will not answer; they shall seek me early, but they shall not find me: For that they hated knowledge, and did not choose the fear of the LORD: They would none of my counsel: they despised all my reproof. Therefore shall they eat of the fruit of their own way, and be filled with their own devices. For the turning away of the simple shall slay them, and the prosperity of fools shall destroy them.* ***But whoso hearkeneth unto me shall dwell safely, and shall be quiet from fear of evil.*** *(Proverbs 1:24-33)*

In Proverbs God also tells us not to fear sudden fear. *Be not afraid (yare':H3372) of sudden fear (pachad: H6343), neither of the desolation of the wicked, when it cometh.* (This is a verse we'd better get in our spirits as 1,000 fall at our side.[15]) *For the LORD shall be thy confidence, and shall keep thy foot from being taken* (captured). *(Proverbs 3:25, 26)* In other words,

[15] Psalms 91:7 *A thousand shall fall at thy side, and ten thousand at thy right hand; but it shall not come nigh thee.*

when legitimate sudden fear comes as a defense mechanism as part of our "fight-or-flight" mechanism, we must not incorporate the experience into either a situational projection or projection into the future and make it a part of our being.

Both fear and fantasy always involves a projection and are very hazardous to our health. What do I mean that they are a projection? When someone fantasizes, they project a thought into:

- a situation and/or
- the future.

A situational fantasy happens when a person daydreams about how a situation could be, rather than what it is. It is when their thoughts actually project themselves into a more enviable position than is reality. For example, many abused children employ fantasy escapism by imagining themselves to be in a peaceful and secure place while being mistreated.

In contrast, a future fantasy is an imagined situation, or even a complete sequence of interactions, occurring out of the context of present time. When this process goes beyond creative thinking and evokes an evil feeling, then we have given an opening to the demons. If the thought of that fantasy is repetitive or always causes the same negative or evil reaction (hate, anger, revenge, pride, etc.) in us, then we can be pretty sure we've been snared.

The situational fantasy often invites greater tentacles of pride and power, while future projections generally give way to the more base emotions of lust, hate, anger, sexual arousal and the like. Finally, fantasy is the playfield of the evil spirits that fragment/divide our soul into schizophrenic personalities under the guise of escapism.

Did you know that certain fantasies are one of the seven abominations to the Lord? *These six things doth the LORD hate: yea, seven are an abomination unto him: A proud look, a lying tongue, and hands that shed innocent blood, An heart that deviseth* ***wicked*** (evil) ***imaginations****,... (Proverbs 6:16-18)*

We have to let God be our Defender instead of creating fantasies that encourage escapism. He will keep us from being captured and snared by our own subconscious and conscious thoughts.[16] Both fantasy and fear focuses upon self and tries to drive us away from trusting or delighting in God.

People become so patterned in negative and fearful thinking that they don't realize what they are doing to themselves. It takes the light of truth from God's Word to open their understanding and overcome the negative and fearful thoughts that they have enthroned. The apostle Paul teaches us that in fighting spiritual battles we are to be, *Casting down imaginations, and every high thing that exalteth itself against the knowledge of God, and bringing into captivity every thought to the obedience of Christ; (2 Corinthians 10:5).* Allow me to cite just a few examples, and how to follow Paul's instruction in spiritual warfare.

Example #1

When my job was eliminated and I didn't know how I was going to make a living, a major media research company sought me out to consult for them. In addition, my former employer granted me a nine month consulting contract! During my first year of "unemployment" I made more money from the severance pay and these two jobs than when I was employed full time. I was very thankful for God's provision, **but** every

[16] See Fear of Evil, pg 33

time I reflected on it, I became worried and greatly fearful about how I would make ends meet next year!

Do you recognize what was happening? Do you discern the pattern? As soon as a thought, especially a good or thankful thought, came to my mind, the enemy within would counter with a worrisome thought about the future (projection). This conscious and subconscious thought would generate a sustaining fear until I literally became "worried sick." The test became: who did I believe? Would I believe and enthrone (submit to) the fear within, or to God and His Word that says: *But my God shall supply all your need according to His riches in glory by Christ Jesus. (Philippians 4:19)* This fearful voice within was a contradiction to God's promise. In order to begin "Overcoming The Fear Within," I had to speak against it and cast this imagination down according to the command of God's Word. In other words, this controlling thought/imagination had to be taken off the ruling throne in my life and replaced with a trust in God's Word and promises.

I had to cut myself off from those thoughts originating from the Tree of Knowledge of Good and Evil which brings death.[17] I had to choose to eat from the Tree of Life – every word proceeding out of the mouth of God, through the Holy Spirit. God's Spirit was renewing my mind by teaching me a new way of thinking – to take captive and cast away every thought that disagreed with the Word of God.

In order for the Body of Christ to do this, we have to allow ourselves to come into a spirit to Spirit relationship with our heavenly Father that is far beyond the reasoning of our mind. If

[17] Genesis 2:17 *But of the tree of the knowledge of good and evil, thou shalt not eat of it: for in the day that thou eatest thereof thou shalt surely die.*

we have fear, then we understand that the mind can be the fertile field of Satan's fruit. In this field the enemy will always try to put the Father's love and His Word in doubt.

When I met my wife-to-be, I didn't just reason that she was attractive, kind, intelligent and would make a good mate on fifteen points of evaluation. No, I began to know her little by little until there was a love relationship and trust established beyond my reasoning.

Men, women and children who have had poor fatherly examples can sometimes find it very difficult to believe or receive the Father's love. However, the bridge to the Father's love can be their love relationship with Jesus and belief in Jesus' Words. Jesus said, *He that hath my commandments, and keepeth them, he it is that loveth me: and he that loveth me shall be loved of my Father, and I will love him, and will manifest myself to him. (John 14:2)* Our heavenly Father loves us – in a spirit-to-Spirit reality beyond man's rational comprehension. He sacrificed His only Son to reconcile us to Himself. What more must our Father do before we realize just how much He truly loves us.

This relationship will allow us to believe, trust and act upon His Word. The singular most important passage I hung onto throughout my learning discipline was: W*e know that all things work together for good to them that love God, to them who are the called according to his purpose. (Romans 8:28)* Because I knew that my heavenly Father loved me, I could hold onto His Word in faith - even in the most agonizing times of spiritual and physical torment. I knew that somehow beyond my understanding, God was performing His will for my good and I could trust Him.

I also knew beyond my reason that I could count on the promises of His Word because my Father would perform His Word even as David wrote of him; *for thou hast magnified thy word above all thy name. (Psalms 138:2)* So if God honored His Word, even above His name, then I just had to grab hold, in faith, to the antidote for the enemies' attacks. The Holy Spirit empowered me to receive, by faith, the Word which would set me free from fear. In this instance, the Lord was trying to get me to trust that He would supply all my monetary needs.[18] It was the Holy Spirit's constant supply of the fruit of faith that drove the spirit of fear from me.

Do you know what has happened? He has supplied all my financial needs – sometimes in the most peculiar, "only God" ways. Additionally, He set me free from the fear of want. It was for my good. When the doctor pulls out a thorn from our flesh, it can hurt! However, *weeping may endure for a night, but joy cometh in the morning. (Psalms 30:5)*

Example #2

A young woman I ministered to was desperately trying to overcome many fears and depression. Although she was beginning to understand and apply the principles contained in the Word, her thought processes kept her in torment. She was thankful for her husband who had been such a wonderful support, but then she would become fearful that something would happen to him (fear of death).

The antidote for her fear was to come into agreement with the Holy Spirit within and speak His Word in order to build up her

---

[18] Philippians 4:19 *But my God shall supply all your need according to his riches in glory by Christ Jesus.*

most holy faith. Such antidotes for the fear of death could be: "Satan, is a liar and the author of my fear." (Romans 8:44 and 2 Timothy 1:7) "Jesus has the keys to hell and of death." (Revelation 1:18) *"Every word of God is pure: he is a shield unto them that put their trust in him." (Proverbs 30:5) "The LORD is my strength and my shield; my heart trusted in him, and I am helped: therefore my heart greatly rejoiceth; and with my song will I praise him."*
(Psalms 28:7)

Example #3
Another mother would thank God for the blessing of her child's good health and immediately fear the child becoming sick tomorrow (fear of illness).

Possible antidotes may include: "I know that my child's *angels do always behold the face of my Father which is in heaven." (Matthew 18:10)* "Jesus *Himself took our infirmities, and bare our sicknesses."* (*Matthew 8:17) "The LORD shall preserve thee* (my child) *from all evil: he shall preserve thy* (my child's) *soul." (Psalms 121:7)*

Notice the similar pattern of the thought processes in each example. Whenever we follow the voice of the Holy Spirit to praise God and think things that are pure, lovely and of a good report,[19] then the fears of our enemies attempt to counter and steal our joy, peace and obedience to the Word. This is a very strong indication that the enemy has a hook in us.

Fear is just like a billboard. When it is in front of us, it demands attention. But when we look away or pass by it, our focus, thoughts and sight go on to what is in front of us. Thus,

---

[19] Philippians 4:8

if we have fear, we have to look to God. We must keep our eyes focused on the truth of the Word, not old RNA responses of our physical being. Take comfort/peace in God and shut down the negative response. This will help create protein syntheses (long term memory responses) that are positive and uplifting. We will be establishing a relationship of greater trust in God, which will release the fruit of faith to annul the spirits of fear operating in our mind and body. This in turn will bring health to the body instead of the fruits of fear which include (but are not limited to):

- shaking, trembling - nausea - hyperventilation

- antihelixes response (dizziness) - muscle tension

- inflammation - panic - hives/itching

- throat closure - fainting - heart arrhythmia

Chapter 4
Summary

1. The antidote for fear is faith – in God and His Word.

2. Faith is a fruit of the Holy Spirit. Fears will be annulled as the faith of the Holy Sprit is released in us.

3. Those obedient to the Word "***shall be quiet from fear of evil.***" *(Proverbs 1:33)*

4. Fear and fantasy always involves a projection into a situation or the future.

5. Fantasy invites sin and some are an abomination to the Lord.

6. Fear produces long-term memory patterns (protein synthesis[20]) that produce varied physiological symptoms in our body.

7. Mixing faith with the Word will bring new long-term memories to make way for restoration of the body's normal functioning.

[20] See Chapter 6 – Physical Timing

Chapter Five

Sanctification

Psalm 91, which we quoted earlier, and several other scriptures[21] contain wonderful assurances for us against the attacks of the enemy and the fear that he puts within our soul. If we, God's people, believe the Word of God is true, then why are so many of His people in fear and under the attacks of the enemy, suffering the fruits of illness that come from it? Could it be that the ecclesia, God's chosen, has little understanding that the truth of the Word has to be apprehended (i.e. appropriated) as well as comprehended just like our salvation?

Let me explain. When we first were born again into the kingdom of God, we had to hear the **good news** of the Word. We had to comprehend or understand the salvation message – the Word of God. However, we were not born into the kingdom of God until, by faith, we **apprehended**, or believed the good news that Jesus died for our sins. Likewise we comprehend the Word that under the shadow of his wings there is great protection. But if we are being destroyed with all types of fears and illnesses (i.e. pestilences) then we haven't apprehended or appropriated the Word of God and/or the conditions for abiding under the shadow of His wings. Jesus did take the curse for us, but we will suffer the consequences of our ignorance and disobedience until we apprehend or appropriate His gift for our daily salvation as well as our eternal salvation.

---

[21] Psalms 118:4,5; Proverbs 1:33; Proverbs 3:24-26; Isaiah 12:2; Isaiah 43:1; Hebrews 13:5,6; etc.

Jesus was crucified as our substitutionary sacrifice in order to reconcile us to God for the sins we have committed. He took the punishment for our sins. In His sacrifice is the provision for our salvation, healing, peace and much more of an abundant life. Jesus' atoning sacrifice was for all mankind, but not all are saved. According to Isaiah 53:5, by the stripes of Jesus' sacrifice "we are healed," but we are not all made well. The same reference says that, "the chastisement of our peace *was* upon him," but we are all not resting in that peace. Jesus is "*the way, the truth, and the* life:" *(John 14:6),* but in faith, we have to apprehend or appropriate the fullness of Him and his provision.

In the beginning of this teaching (page 17) Proverbs 1:24-31 taught us that the reason we receive fear into our lives is our distant relationship with God and disobedience to His Word. How long will we continue to walk in our ignorance of the evidence of fear that tears us apart inside? We have to begin realizing and accept that God is trying to sanctify the temples of his chosen ones to make us whole, holy (like He is holy) and Christ-like. In this day, our Heavenly Father is disciplining his children with fire to separate the dross from us.

We believe and declare that: ***All scripture*** *is given by inspiration of God, and is profitable for doctrine, for reproof, for correction,* ***for instruction in righteousness****: That the man of God may be perfect, thoroughly furnished unto all good works. (2 Timothy 3:16)* Yet, the modern church discounts the Old Testament Word, not realizing that the Old Testament was the only "scripture" when Paul wrote this to Timothy! The New Testament was not yet written! We can quote that our Lord is the same yesterday, today and forever (Hebrews 13:8), but under the new covenant ignore the Lord's sameness in the Old

Testament's "instructions in righteousness." We ignore the way the Lord allowed Satan to affect the righteous man, Job, in order to purge him from pride and give him a greater revelation of God. We ignore the instructions of demanded obedience given to his chosen people, Israel. However, we will try to claim the promises and blessings that come from that obedience. It is time for the Body of Christ to embrace the whole truth. It is time that we seek God and listen to what the Spirit is saying.

Listen to the Word as God talks about how He will purify His own: *The sinners in Zion* (his people, the saved, the ecclesia, the church) *are afraid; fearfulness hath surprised the hypocrites. (Isaiah 33:14)* What are we when we say we love God and don't? What are we when we say we trust God and don't? What are we when we say we love our neighbor and slander him? We're a hypocrite who, according to this scripture, will have **fearfulness. The origin of all fear is that we don't trust and obey God.** If one doesn't trust God it means that they don't have a right relationship with the Holy Spirit. Instead of hearing and receiving faith from the Holy Spirit, they listen to the spirit of fear. When they embrace that fear, they are open to God's judgments of even greater delusions and greater lies. They can go from fear to panic and manifest stress, anxiety, and "dis-ease" resulting in oppression, depression, and various diseases.

Let's read that verse again and continue: *The sinners in Zion are afraid; fearfulness hath surprised the hypocrites. Who among us shall dwell with the devouring fire? Who among us shall dwell with everlasting burnings? (Isaiah 33:14)* God is sanctifying His church and unless we obey and trust Him we will feel the fire of His cleansing. What is that fire? It is the fire of the testing of our faith that tests our love and obedience to Jesus Christ. This is the fire that will consume anything in us that is ungodly, including fear. Remember, God says He is preparing His bride without spot, wrinkle or blemish. Isn't that what Zion is experiencing? This verse continues to give us, Zion, the answer. *He that* ***walketh righteously****, and* ***speaketh uprightly****; he that despiseth the gain of oppressions, that shaketh his hands from holding of bribes, that stoppeth his ears from hearing of blood, and shutteth his eyes from seeing evil; He shall dwell on high: his place of defence shall be the munitions of rocks: bread shall be given him; his waters shall be sure. Thine eyes shall see the king in his beauty: they shall behold the land that is very far off... (Isaiah 33:15-17)*

The gospel of Matthew says it this way: *Blessed are the pure in heart: for they shall see God. (Matthew 5:8)*

Luke 21:26 tells us that as God shakes the heavens, fear will cause the hearts of men to fail, but he who **walks** righteously can dwell within the burnings - beholding the glory of the Lord. Now that's truly dwelling under the shadow of His wings! That's having the defense of **the** Rock of my salvation and being sustained in His presence ("bread") and full of the Spirit ("his waters shall be sure"). What a glorious position – and promise! However, let us take note that we don't just acquire this status. We must **walk** righteously. That is something we must do, it is not an acquired position in its fullness at the time of our salvation to eternal life. It is acquired (and sustained) progressively as we walk righteously.

This walk of righteousness is not according to our deceptive reasoning which has been conformed to this world: but by the transformation and the renewing of our minds (Romans 12:2) through the washing of the water of the Word. (Ephesians 5:26) We must choose to be led by the Holy Spirit and not our own way. Our hearts must be in position so we can obey. Paul again referred to this true walk of righteousness in his letter to the Philippians, when he exhorts them to "work out their own salvation."[22]

The Lord repeats His admonishment and refers to the fear and delusion that He will allow upon His people in the sixty sixth chapter of Isaiah. He is talking to His people about the repulsiveness of their ceremonial religious practices while their hearts were in disobedience and out of communion with him: *...Yea, they have chosen their own ways, and their soul delighteth in their abominations. I also will choose their delusions, and will bring their fears upon them; because when I called, none did answer; when I spake, they did not hear: but they did evil before mine eyes, and chose that in which I delighted not* ***Hear the word of the LORD, ye that tremble at his word****; (Isaiah 66:3-5)*

Remember faith comes by hearing and hearing by the Word of God. This is the hour that the Holy Spirit is calling us to **hear** and **obey** God. We must choose to cut ourselves off from the enemies' voices that speak lies and lead us down the road of destruction.

In this critical time, before Jesus' return to rule and reign on earth, the Lord is sanctifying His church. Today, Zion is being called to throw off the religious form and enter into a meaningful and perfect love relationship with our Lord. Do we want to be free from fear? Then we must learn from the evidence of our disciplining that we are not walking uprightly. We simply must learn to trust and obey the Lord by the leading of the Holy Spirit out of the love we have for Him.

[22] Philippians 2:12

The 28th chapter of Deuteronomy, beginning in verse 58, also tells us why we take fear upon ourselves and where fear (and resulting disease) comes from. Let's read it with understanding for our own lives. *If thou wilt not observe to do all the words of this law that are written in this book, that thou mayest fear*[23] *this glorious and fearful name, THE LORD THY GOD; Then the LORD will make thy plagues wonderful,*[24] *and the plagues of thy seed,* (YOUR CHILDREN, THROUGH GENERATIONAL HERITAGES) even great plagues, and of long continuance (LINGERING ILLNESS), *and sore sicknesses, and of long continuance. Moreover he will bring upon thee all the diseases of Egypt, which thou wast afraid of* (FEAR OF DISEASE); *and they shall cleave unto thee.* (This includes fear itself.) *Also every sickness, and every plague, which is not written in the book of this law, them will the LORD bring upon thee, until thou be destroyed. And ye shall be left few in number, whereas ye were as the stars of heaven for multitude; because thou wouldest not obey the voice of the LORD thy God.* (FEAR NOT, TRUST GOD, OBEY GOD, FORGIVE, TRUST NOT IN MAN, ETC.) *And it shall come to pass, that as the LORD rejoiced over you to do you good, and to multiply you; so the LORD will rejoice over you to destroy you, and to bring you to nought; and ye shall be plucked from off the land whither thou goest to possess it. And the LORD shall scatter thee among all people, from the one end of the earth even unto the other; and there thou shalt serve other gods, which neither thou nor thy fathers have known, even wood and stone. And among these nations shalt thou find no ease, neither shall the sole of thy foot have rest: but the LORD shall give thee there a trembling heart (ANXIETY), and failing of eyes* (FAILING EYESIGHT), *and sorrow of mind* (DEPRESSION): *And thy life shall hang in doubt before thee; and thou shalt fear*

[23] Hebrew: *yare'* – to revere. This is reverential "fear," NOT demonic fear.
[24] Hebrew: *pala'* – distinguished or singularly hard, difficult

day and night, and shalt have none assurance of thy life (FEAR OF DEATH): *In the morning thou shalt say, Would God it were even! and at even thou shalt say, Would God it were morning! for the fear of thine* ***heart*** *wherewith thou shalt fear, and for the sight of thine eyes which thou shalt see.* (YOU FEAR EVERYTHING YOU SEE). *And the LORD shall bring thee into Egypt* (BONDAGE) *again with ships, by the way*[25] (COURSE OF LIFE) *whereof I spake unto thee, Thou shalt see it no more again: and there* ***ye shall be sold unto your enemies*** *for bondmen and bondwomen, and* ***no man shall buy you****.* *(Deuteronomy 28:58-68)*

This last scripture makes it all so obvious that God is speaking on a spiritual dimension. For how can you be "sold unto your enemies" and be "bondmen and bondwomen" when no man will buy you?! In order to be "sold" when "no man will buy you," is it not obvious that God is speaking about us "selling" our soul to something that is not flesh and blood? We "sell" our souls to these evil spirits.

The Bible was written to and for the edification of the church (the ecclesia); those called-out people of God before and after Christ's resurrection. I am not advocating that we go into works of legalism in following the commandments of God. However, is legalism seeking to please the Father by strictly adhering to His commands? No, it is not. Legalism is when someone else insists that you follow their interpretation of God's commands and instructions.

Even the first council of elders at Jerusalem commanded the new gentile converts to adhere to only the rudimentary elements of "Moses' law." It was, in fact, that part of the Mosaic Law which would make them socially acceptable to Jewish believers.

---

[25] Hebrew: *derek* – course of life or road of action

Specifically, they were to abstain from idols, fornication, things strangled and blood. The reason why the council came to agreement of only commanding them to honor these few "laws" was because they believed that the Word would be received by the converts "in the synagogues every Sabbath day."[26]

I'm not saying that we must follow all the pharisaical and rabbinical interpretations of the "Jewish laws" in order to obtain eternal life. However, I am saying that there are spiritual principles of disobedience to God's Word and His commandments, which affect our health and personal righteousness. It is an individual choice if we want to live abundantly in victory or live in weakness, infirmity, agony and defeat by ignoring the commands of the Word. Jesus said that he didn't come to throw out the laws of His Word.[27] His Word says, *I call heaven and earth to record this day against you, that I have set before you life and death, blessing and cursing: therefore choose life, that both thou and thy seed may live: That thou mayest* ***love the LORD thy God, and that thou mayest obey his voice****, and that thou mayest cleave unto him: for He is thy life, and the length of thy days:...(Deuteronomy 30:19, 20)* So we have a choice – blessings or curses. Which will we choose, love and obedience, or fear and disease?

I am pleading with the entire body of Christ that we begin moving toward a renewed washing of the water of the Word; and that we do this in obedience to His instructions and teachings unto sanctification and His righteousness. We must

---

[26] Acts 15:21 *For Moses of old time hath in every city them that preach him, being read in the synagogues every Sabbath do.*

[27] Matthew 5:17 (NIV) *Do not think that I have come to abolish the Law or the Prophets; I have not come to abolish them but to fulfill them.*

quit soiling our garments of righteousness and "walk in white." *Thou hast a few names even in Sardis* (believers) *which have not defiled their garments; and they shall walk with me in white: for they are worthy. (Revelation 3:4)* These garments are the fine white linen of the bride which is the righteousness of the saints: *And to her was granted that she should be arrayed in fine linen, clean and white: for the fine linen is the righteousness of saints. (Revelation 19:8)*

Jesus said, *If a person* ***really loves*** *me he will keep my word [obey my teaching]; and my Father will love him, and* ***We*** *will come to him and make Our home (abode, special dwelling place) with him. (John 14:23 Amplified Bible)* When we are in obedience, He who is perfect love will manifest or reveal himself and abide with us. Then **our fear will not be able to remain** because, *There is no fear in love; but perfect love casteth out fear: because fear hath torment. (1 John 4:18)*

Let those who have ears to hear; hear what the Spirit is saying. *For the eyes of the LORD run to and fro throughout the whole earth, to show himself strong in the behalf of them whose heart is perfect toward him. (2 Chronicles 16:9)* Will you "really love" Him with perfect love? There is freedom from the torment of fear. Receive it with thankfulness of heart. He loves you.

Three Dimensions of Victory

You can – and must – defeat these spirits of fear on three dimensions:

1. Knowing the truth – *And ye shall know the truth, and the truth shall make you free. (John 8:32)*

2. Obeying God (relationship with God) and resisting the devil.

3. Casting out of evil spirits – (A person must have the knowledge as well as the determination not to allow re-entry. Pray for greater discernment to see the traps that are being laid.)

1. Knowing the Truth

The truth is that God is greater than the devil and his demons. *Finally, my brethren, be strong* ***in the Lord****, and in the power of* ***his*** *might. If God be for you, who can be against you. (Ephesians 6:10)* God has made provision for our freedom in His Word. What we consistently have to do is receive knowledge and understanding of it, edify ourselves in the Word, and **believe that Word** so the devil can't destroy us. God will not leave us. Now that we are getting enlightenment through knowledge, will we begin walking in a greater trust of God and His Word? The Word has power when it is mixed with faith. For when it is not mixed with faith, there is neither eternal nor daily salvation. *For unto us was the gospel preached, as well as unto them: but the word preached did not profit them, not being mixed with faith in them that heard it. (Hebrews 4:2) Put on the whole armour of God, that ye may be able to stand against the wiles* (methods) *of the devil. (Ephesians 6:11)* Is this something that God does or something we have to do? It is something we have to do.

We are in a war! *For we wrestle not against flesh and blood, but against principalities, against powers, against the rulers of the darkness of this world, against spiritual wickedness in high places. (Ephesians 6:12)* In this verse "wrestle" is the Greek word *pale* (G3823) which is from *pallo* (G906), meaning "to

cast" as in "cast down." We have been ordered to cast down all imaginations/thoughts that are against the Word of God. Thus, we must continuously cast down all these spirits that express themselves as imaginations that bring us into bondage. We have been given a command and the authority to cast the demons and their input down, underneath our feet. *Behold, I give unto you power to tread on serpents and scorpions, and over all the power of the enemy:..*
(Luke 10:19)

2. Obeying God

Be not deceived; God is not mocked: for whatsoever a man soweth, that shall he also reap. For he that soweth to his flesh shall of the flesh reap corruption; but he that soweth to the Spirit shall of the Spirit reap life everlasting. ("Life everlasting means continuously, both now and in the future, forever.) ***And let us not be weary in well doing: for in due season we shall reap, if we faint not.*** *(Gal 6:7-9)* We are not in a war to always be warring as a way of religious activity, but we are in a war to become free and become the people of God He's called us to be. We are in a war to receive the rest that God has promised and prepared for us. We need to work and fight for our freedom and greater faith. As we go from faith to faith, strength to strength, and glory to glory we are being changed into someone (the bride) without spot or blemish – Christ-like.

But we all, with open face beholding as in a glass the glory of the Lord, ***are changed into the same image from glory to glory****, even as by the Spirit of the Lord.* (2 *Corinthians 3:18)*

If it is the finger of God, the Spirit of the Lord, that changes us and casts out demons, don't we have to be always mindful not to offend or reject the Holy Spirit? When the Holy Spirit tries to enlighten our darkness, our rejection and offense toward Him will cause us to miss the opportunities of spiritual growth and the calling for our lives. We will not only miss growth opportunities, our increased hardness of heart will lengthen the time of our torment under fear as we push Him further away from our lives.

3. Casting Out Evil Spirits

Let me say it again. Our warfare should be when the Spirit calls us and what He calls us to do. We are not to engage in ritualistic warfare just for the sake of being "spiritual" or stirring up our soul. Engaging in spiritual warfare for the sake of being seen as a warrior is a religious manifestation that invites demonic religious spirits. We are to wrestle with the enemy in the power of the Holy Spirit in order to overcome and have victory. As our faith is, so it will be unto us.

How do we do this? *Casting down imaginations, and every high thing that exalteth itself against the knowledge of God, and bringing into captivity every thought to the obedience of Christ; And having in a* ***readiness*** *to revenge all disobedience*, **when (or after)** ***your obedience is fulfilled.*** *(2 Corinthians 10:5,6)* We can not have power over the devil unless we are obedient to God – in thought, word, and deed. ***Submit*** *yourselves therefore to God.* ***Resist*** *the devil, and* ***he will flee*** *from you. (James 4:7)* We cannot be double minded in trusting or obeying God. In other words we must practice faith (trusting the Word) and obey God continuously. We can't allow ourselves to become a revolving door for spirits of Satan's kingdom. Speaking, standing upon, or doing the Word and building ourselves up in our most holy faith can't be like a light switch to turn on and off or we will be deceived into thinking we are in obedience, when we are not. It must be a consistent seeking of His face – who He is – this is relationship.

The Decision Gap

At the prompting of the Holy Spirit, I have often advised people of a strange sensation that they might encounter following expulsion of their fears. Let me give you a little understanding of what I've often referred to as the "decision gap."

We said that "pachad" (H6343) was the "sudden alarm to an object or stimulus." By implication it is a feeling. Is fear just a thought? No! Ask anyone who has had fear. It is a feeling. So do you always <u>think</u> yourself to fear or do you sometimes <u>feel</u> the fear in your belly/body cavity? This is not just "nerves," this is one or more spirits.

When people receive deliverance from fear do they lose the memory? No! The same video tape is running in their mind. However, the feeling of anxiety which the spirit caused is gone. It is as if there is an opportunity of time or a "gap for decision" whether or not we will form a new protein synthesis (long term memory) or reinforce the old. With the evil spirit gone, there is no longer the communication with our mind to secrete these stabilizing body chemicals, so there is a gap. It is like our mind is waiting for direction. In those moments there is a "decision gap" until we have planted a more perfect way of thinking (I speak in faith). That "gap" will actually disappear over time. It disappears because, hopefully, we have replaced that fear with God's Word and a new way of thinking.

A few years ago, I received a letter from a woman who was released from a spirit of irritation. Her account may help us to understand how this "gap" phenomenon is experienced when God delivers us from fears.

> "As you mentioned, the Lord has given me a "pause button" or a "moment of decision." The choice is still mine, but I feel that it is easier to make the right choice most of the time because the Holy Spirit is directing and guiding me. In these past few days when adverse situations are going on what I feel I have received is a greater sense of a "trigger" or an "alarm" within my spirit, but not the spirit of irritation rising up. It is discernment and not a "rising up within me. It is as if that "pause" button has gotten longer and it really isn't difficult (most of the time) to fight it."

Now then, are these disembodied spirits totally ineffective? No, they are not. They will come back to check the house and challenge our thinking. HOWEVER, they don't subliminally touch our mind-body connector <u>unless we allow</u> them to re-establish a beach-head through our sin and re-acceptance of our fears. Jesus said it this way: *When the unclean spirit is gone out of a man, he walketh through dry places, seeking rest; and finding none, he saith, <u>I will return unto my house</u> whence I came out. And when he cometh, he findeth it swept and garnished. Then goeth he, and taketh to him seven other spirits more wicked than himself; and they enter in, and dwell there: and the last state of that man is worse than the first. (Luke 11:24-26)*

Please note two things from this passage. First, when the unclean spirit is cast out, after a time, he will come back to inspect his former dwelling. Then if, and only if, he finds it empty, will he come back to dwell. We can not leave our house cleaned and decorated in religious ceremony. In order to prevent re-entry of the spirit and his entourage, we absolutely must have it filled with the Holy Spirit and His sword – the Word of God. Then, our thought patterns can come into alignment with the Word and we can *cast down imaginations, and every high thing that exalteth itself against the knowledge of God, and bring into captivity every thought to the obedience of Christ. (2 Corinthians 10:5)*

Another marvelous thing happens once we are set free from fears. When the evil spirit does come back to check the house, our body often acts like a Geiger counter to alert us to its presence. The spirit may well be on the outside, but our racing heart, shortness of breath, clamminess, tightened throat, and every fiber in our body can give us discernment of its approach, even when we are not in (agreement with) fear. It can be an alert saying that now is the time to speak the Words of warfare and resist the attack. For as the scriptures say if we have humbled ourselves[28] before God and resist the devil, he will flee from us. *Submit yourselves therefore to God. Resist the devil, and he will flee from you. (James 4:7)*

[28] See Chapter 9

Chapter 5
Summary

1. By faith, we have to apprehend (believe and appropriate) as well as comprehend (understand) God's Word for it to be effective in our lives.

2. This is the day that God is sanctifying His church with the fires of His testings to rid us of the dross within our hearts.

3. The origin of all fear is our:
   - lack of trust in, and
   - disobedience to God.

4. The ecclesia is being called to:
   - throw off contrived, ceremonial religious practices and enter a pure love relationship with Him.
   - wash our bridal garments by walking in righteousness.

5. When freedom from fear is manifest, there is often a "decision gap" that allows new opportunity to make correct choices.

Chapter Six

Timing

Let me address one of the most difficult issues that we have to deal with as we walk out of our fears. That issue is timing. We are often desperate for the Lord's instant healing hand. He often does exactly that and gives us miraculous, instantaneous healing. However, when the symptoms of our body continue, we are tempted to lose our faith, our resolve and our walk because we really don't understand God and the spiritual realm or our body in the physical realm.

Spiritual Timing

*Humble yourselves therefore under the mighty hand of God, that he may exalt you in **due time**: (1 Peter 5:6)*

Teaching of the Word brings forth faith and knowledge, so that we don't perish. (2 Peter 1:5) When I was first learning how to walk in this spiritual kingdom, the Holy Spirit urged me to take the Word of God and beat on the devil in faith, by speaking forth specific scriptures. Then, I had to allow for the "due time" to pass so that the spirits of fear would be revealed and expelled. If we will do that, then symptoms of trembling, pain and disease within the body will disappear. If we do not allow God's season in our expectation, we do not develop patience, and we give fear a chance to come back and point to symptoms. Having done all, **stand**! We must wait for fruit from the planting to come forth in <u>God's season</u> and not our expectations or out of a spirit of pity, condemnation, accusation, etc. We can't allow premature expectations to become another opening for the devil to work destruction in other areas.

Whether our thinking is clear or foggy or we're feeling good or poorly today, should not affect our stand in faith. Fear drives us to strife and striving, but patience/perseverance yields the fruit of godliness. In speaking of adding to our faith Peter said, *And to knowledge temperance* (self control)*; and to temperance patience* (perseverance)*; and to patience godliness;(2 Peter 1:6)*

And let us not be weary in well doing: ***for in due season we shall reap****, if we faint not. For he that soweth to his flesh shall of the flesh reap corruption; but he that soweth to the Spirit shall of the Spirit reap life everlasting. (Galatians 6:8,9)*

We have not been programmed to fear. There is a difference between thought and instinct. Unlike animals that God made with imprinted instincts, humans don't have instinctive learning. We have demons that sin gave an entryway to; either through our forefathers' sin or our own. We learn from either transference of spirits from the womb (generational curses) or from our own experiences. An example of this is colic in a baby. It is believed that colic is the result of a transferred fear from the mother to the baby sometime in pregnancy. What produces the hormonal excretions to cause colic? – FEAR.

In us, fear is a killer. Medical science now says that when fear and its resulting anxiety and stress are existent, you're in as much danger of heart problems, as having high cholesterol or smoking. Fear directly affects nerve actions, impulses and the sympathetic nervous system. Some leading authorities believe that migraines are rooted in guilt and out of guilt comes fear and self hatred. Let's examine how these physical affects come to be and consider the physical timing at the same time.

Physical Timing

Background:

Long-term memory is an impression – an electro chemical action that happens within the brain and creates protein synthesis – the putting together of a complex mixture of proteins. Protein synthesis produces a genetic component called RNA - ribonucleic acid. This then, becomes part of your biological makeup. So, some thoughts, even at the subconscious level, produce the same biological/physical reactions as the learning that produced those reactions initially.

Let me say that again in a more understandable, non-medical language: When we have had a traumatic experience, physical or psychological, that invokes a fearful reaction, it can become a consistent chemical reaction by projecting that thought into the future. For example when I fell off a thirty foot ladder, I experienced trauma. The "feet" or base of the ladder was not secure and slipped away from the house. My weight on the top of the ladder continued to push the base further and further away while the top of the ladder and I slipped down and down until it reached the overhang at the fifteen foot level. Then, the ladder and I, crashed through the pine tree and onto the bushes and ground below. I was scratched, bruised, stunned and in pain.

The next time I had to use that ladder I remembered the trauma it had caused and for a second I became clammy, somewhat fearful and my legs began to quiver as I started to ascend. Now, I had a choice. I could either use the Word of God and allow the Holy Spirit to overcome my fear, or I could put the ladder away until I "got my fear under control." If I had chosen the latter option and projected that experience into the future when I would have to use the ladder again, I would have had an even greater difficulty. The more frequently I would have allowed that fear to dominate, the more fixed it would have become in my long term memory (protein synthesis) and associated bodily reactions.

In other words, if I took that traumatic experience and projected it into the future, then the ladder is no longer just a tool to use with wisdom and caution. Just the sight of it would cause me to shake. I could have become irrationally fearful of the object or situation (that's a phobia) and project it from my one painful experience of falling off the ladder. Once implanted into the body's chemical reactions, I become one with the thought and/or the demonic spirit to which the projection of that fear gave an opening. This in turn could establish the fearful thinking pattern and a consistent state of alarm every time I saw or thought about a ladder.

(Thankfully, I did not choose that alternative. Instead, I faced my fear with God's Word and comfortably used the ladder – with an anchor at the base! That is wisdom, not fear.)

The Conflict:

Now you have a new spiritual insight that "God has not given you a spirit of fear" in direct conflict with what your body is doing to you. What do you do? You have to make new long-term memories and associations – new protein synthesis – that stay with you in your soul/body. Long-term memory stays with you by reinforcement. If you repeatedly fear a thing, it will reinforce memory and the resultant bodily reactions. However, if we repeatedly use the Word in faith to overcome our fear, then we will develop a non threatening long term memory and its resultant "normal" or even edified bodily reactions. We will become and feel "free" and "alive!" In other words, we have to repeatedly apply the Word, *That He might sanctify and cleanse it* (the church, i.e. us) *with the washing of water by the word. (Ephesians 5:26)*

Is this process scriptural or a method of man? It is the teaching of Jesus. Paul explained it this way: (Using the Amplified Bible to bring out the meaning.) In Ephesians 4:17 Paul begins by making a contrast between the walk of a heathen gentile and the walk of a believing doer of the Word. *So this I say and solemnly testify in the name of the Lord, that you must no longer live as the heathen do in the perverseness (vanity and futility) of their minds. Their moral understanding is darkened and their reasoning is beclouded, alienated and estranged from the life of God* (AND HIS BLESSINGS) *because of the ignorance that is deep-seated in them, due to their hardness of heart* (I'LL DO IT MY WAY). *In their spiritual apathy they have become callous and past feeling, abandoning themselves as a prey to unbridled sensuality, eager and greedy to indulge in every form of impurity that their depraved* ***desires** suggest and demand. But you did not so learn Christ! Assuming that you have really heard Him and been taught by Him, as all Truth is in Jesus, Strip yourselves of your former nature discard your old unrenewed self which is characterized by your previous manner of life* (THOUGHTS AND DEEDS) *and becomes corrupt through lusts and desires that spring from delusions. And be constantly renewed in the spirit of your mind –* ***having a new mental and spiritual attitude.*** *And* ***put on the new nature****, the regenerated self, created in God's image, in true righteousness and holiness. Therefore, rejecting all falsity and being done now with it, let everyone express the truth* (WHAT

IS TRUTH? "THY WORD IS TRUTH."), *with his neighbor for we are all parts of one body and members one of another. (Ephesians 4:17-23)* (Bolding and parenthetical capitalization added by author.)

In other words, we are to replace the old thoughts that are reinforced by the fearful demon with the truth of the good news brought by Jesus.

Do we completely lose the old memories? No! It is like pain. We remember having the pain of injuries, but unless spirits are involved with fear or phantom pains, we don't have the same pain anymore. Thus, we have both new and old memories within us at the same time. So then, as Paul taught; *When I was a child, I spake as a child, I understood as a child, I thought as a child: but when I became a man* (became mature), *I put away childish things. (1 Corinthians 13:11)* Just like childhood thoughts and memories, you no longer choose to think as a child, but as an adult, in agreement with the Holy Spirit and faith in the Word of God. We must choose to examine every thought and let go of those that do not line up with God's standard (Holy Bible).

As we choose the new, more and more often *Casting down imaginations, and every high thing that exalteth itself against the knowledge of God, and bringing into captivity every thought to the obedience of Christ; (2 Corinthians 10:5)* it becomes a new way of life within our being. It is the new way that produces different RNA and fruit of the Spirit of God – like love, joy and peace.[29]

---

[29] Galatians 5:22 *But the fruit of the Spirit is love, joy, peace, longsuffering, gentleness, goodness, faith, meekness, temperance:..*

While you are under the torment of fears, the enemy will squash your fruit. I always thought I was a very blessed and a relatively happy person. But when fears had their grip upon me I was not only physically miserable, I lost all my joy for living. This left me open for other attacking spirits like depression, suicide, self pity and the like. I had to walk around the block and sing, "This is the Day that the Lord has made. I will rejoice and be glad in it," over and over again in order to get any relief from the oppression that overwhelmed me. Every day I walked and sang, "I will rejoice and be glad in it." By the 10th or 20th time I sang it each day, I actually learned through feeling better, that there was power in my words of praise.

One day a missionary pastor came by the house to visit my mother-in-law who was recovering from a broken femur bone. On the way out the door he said to me that my time of testing will pass and there will be a renewed joy of the Spirit within me. At the time he said that, he may as well have been talking to a diseased Elm tree, because I was so dead, stiff and full of self-pity, I could only nod courteously for the misery I was in. But God is so gracious to us, and the man's words came true. Oh yes, I can whole heartedly testify that the fruit of the Spirit does return – in due season – as we are obedient in faith to the Word of God.

As a matter of fact, it was in ministering to others that my joy returned. The last stages of my restoration were accomplished through the joy of ministering. Doesn't the Word tell us that a happy heart is good medicine? *A merry heart doeth good like a medicine: but a broken spirit drieth the bones. (Proverbs 17:22)* Even though I didn't always feel like ministering with the little I had to give, my spirit was being renewed as I did so. I was being obedient to the command: *Freely you have received, freely give. (Mat 10:8 NIV)* I believe that God honored my obedience to His Spirit's leading.

Slowly, I was experiencing a whole new revelation and reality of God's kingdom principles through the Holy Spirit. I was being disconnected from my way of thinking that brought death to my body, soul and spirit. Instead of walking by sight in my misery and fears, the Holy Spirit was teaching me how to walk in faith by His Word. Out of my love for Him, I had prayed as David: *Create in me a clean heart, O God; and renew a right spirit within me. Cast me not away from thy presence; and take not thy holy spirit from me. Restore unto me the joy of thy salvation; and uphold me with thy free spirit. (Psalms 51:10-12)* God was answering my prayers, but not the way I had expected!

Although we can't erase all the old memories (protein synthesis), we can choose the new, more perfect way of Jesus even in the times of trial. When we've been ignorant and then receive knowledge, does the wise man choose to continue in ignorance - knowing that it will destroy him? No! Likewise, we must choose to be informed and follow God's "new" way.

So then, when we choose the new way, old long term memories cease to produce the intensity of RNA (ribonucleic acid). Excessive RNA is no longer pumped through our bloodstream to cause us to "feel" the affects of fear; like trembling, panic, shaking, etc. When does this happen? When we replace the <u>old man</u> with the <u>new man's</u> thinking and bind it, by faith, into our very being. This is the "due season" during which we "stand fast" in faith and wait. This harvest can be immediate, but sometimes symptoms can continue for a very long time.

As I shared in the introduction of this book, I was tormented for nearly two years before the Lord taught me how to overcome my fears. During that time, these evil spirits took a great toll on my body as my immune system deteriorated and my nervous system was attacked continuously. One of the symptoms that stayed with me for more than three years after the expulsion of the spirits was a shaking or tremor in my torso and arms when I awoke. To touch me was like touching a vibrating machine set on "high." I quivered awake almost every morning and most often during the night as well. As a result, discouragement and the fear of re-entry was constantly staring me in the face.

Medical practitioners, or any whiplash victim, will say that damage to the nerves and nervous system generally require the longest recovery times. Lingering manifestations can cause you to doubt the deliverance you're received and make you feel unclean and discouraged. However, you must continue to stand upon the Word in your most holy faith. The time may seem interminable, but one day you too will finally awake rested, realizing that the symptom didn't manifest this day. Then for a little while it may come and go as your daily life brings forth new stresses or anxieties to overcome. However, as you continue walking in obedience, trusting Abba Father and His Word, you too may be almost surprised to one day realize that there are no more residual affects.

I am one person who truly understands that it is very difficult to stand and bear up in faith when you don't "feel" the presence of God through the torment and pain. However, as we patiently spend time in faith, dying to ourselves and our old thoughts, the Word promises that it is for our ultimate good. God leads us beyond this fruit of patience unto godliness of our character.[30]

[30] 2 Peter 1:6 *And to knowledge temperance; and to temperance patience; and to patience godliness;*

Let me say that again so that we may take hope in discouraging times of waiting for God's hand to move on our behalf. While God is delivering us from the spirits of fear, through our faith and obedience to Him, He is also growing the fruit of godliness through patience in us. As our old thought processes wane and become those of the mature "new man" in Christ, our RNA secretions return to normal and so does our body. Then, we are able to walk in the completed freedom of our salvation. This is the freedom not to sin and the freedom to walk in obedience to the Word of God. *You were taught, with regard to your former way of life, to put off your old self, which is being corrupted by its deceitful desires; to be made new in the attitude of your minds; and to put on the new self, created to be like God in true righteousness and holiness. (Ephesians 4:22-24 NIV)*

Chapter 6
Summary

1. The Holy Spirit reveals knowledge of the Word to prepare us for deliverance.

2. The season of our freedom is in God's "due time" or "in season."

3. Physical restoration requires the re-establishment of "normal" RNA secretions in response to the thoughts and choices of the "new man" in Christ.

4. Damaged nerves generally require longer healing times than bodily functions.

5. The time we spend standing in faith brings forth patience unto godliness.

Chapter Seven

From Our Hearts

Thoughts and Words

We've talked a lot about the need to replace our evil and destructive thinking with the truth of the Word of God in order to put new patterns of thought in our heads and hearts. Let us now consider how our words impact our thoughts and freedom.

And when they bring you unto the synagogues, and unto magistrates, and powers, take ye no thought how or what thing ye shall answer, or what ye shall say: For the Holy Ghost shall teach you in the same hour what ye ought to say.
(Luke 12:11,12)

We need to pause before we speak, to allow the Holy Spirit to give us an answer rather than our ruling fears or the kingdom of sin.

Our words demand a response and fulfillment. That's why we must be careful what we speak. Out of the heart of man proceeds every evil thing. Our words reflect our heart. *O generation of vipers, how can ye, being evil, speak good things? for out of the abundance of the heart the mouth speaketh. (Matthew 12:34)* It is what we believe in our heart that brings life or death to us. *That if thou shalt confess with thy mouth the Lord Jesus, and shalt believe in thine heart that God hath raised him from the dead, thou shalt be saved. For with the heart man believeth unto righteousness; and with the mouth confession is made unto salvation. (Rom 10:9,10)* It is the belief in our heart, which motivates our confession – good or bad.

We also need to watch our words and be careful not to curse someone else. Forgive so you can be forgiven. Did you ever wonder why Jacob's beloved Rachel died? Could it be that she died prematurely because Jacob cursed her with a curse of death. When Laban came for his idols which Rachel had hid, Jacob said let the one who stole them die![31] Our words are powerful! However, let's not take fear from someone else's cursing words for the Word says: *Like a fluttering sparrow or a darting swallow, an undeserved curse does not come to rest. (Proverbs 26:2 NIV)*

If your heart's belief can bring you righteousness, and confession unto salvation, then what can our evil heart's belief do when we confess that?! Our mouths can give us life or death – it is in the power of our beliefs and mouth. *Death and life are in the power of the tongue: (Proverbs 18:21)*

Jesus said, *But I say unto you, That every idle word that men shall speak, they shall give account thereof in the day of judgment.* ***For by thy words thou shalt be justified, and by thy words thou shalt be condemned.*** Do you hear the words of Jesus? ***For by thy words thou shalt be justified, and by thy words thou shalt be condemned.*** *(Matthew 12:36,37)*

The scriptures teach us that the thoughts in our hearts will manifest either by deed or speech. ***We having the same spirit***

[31] Genesis 31:32 *With whomsoever thou findest thy gods, let him not live: before our brethren discern thou what is thine with me, and take it to thee. For Jacob knew not that Rachel had stolen them.*

of faith, according as it is written, I believed, and therefore have I spoken; we also believe, and therefore speak; (2 Corinthians 4:13)

Words of Slander

Just as our words can bring life or death to us, so can our words bring blessings or curses on others. If we genuinely speak well of someone, they are encouraged. However, if we speak evil of another, the scriptures not only call us a fool,[32] but say that our words are our destruction and snare to our soul![33] Additionally, if there is an opening to the soul of the person we slander, we can bring fear, terror, and trembling upon them. Our words can be an instrument of blessing and life, or an instrument of murder and death.

Many Christians have received a fear of slander by the accusations of a brother or sister in Christ. *Because of the voice of the enemy, because of the oppression of the wicked: for they cast iniquity upon me, and in wrath they hate me. My heart is sore pained within me: and the terrors of death are fallen upon me. Fearfulness and trembling are come upon me, and horror hath overwhelmed me. (Psalms 55:3-5)* That is why it is so very important to forgive each other. If we are able to forgive, then there is no sin laid to our charge. Without sin, there is no opening for the enemy to put fear upon us.

---

[32] Proverbs 10:18 *He that hideth hatred with lying lips, and he that uttereth a slander, is a fool.*
[33] Proverbs 18:7 *A fool's mouth is his destruction, and his lips are the snare of his soul.*

Dimensions of Thought

There are two dimensions of evil thought. There is temptation and then there is the evil that lives within us – or the actuality of sin which is a part of us. [*All these evil things come from within, and defile the man. (Mark 7:23)*] The devil will tempt us with our own thoughts. This is especially evidenced by the dominating thoughts of rationalization, justification and logic in our lives. However, temptation to fear is not sin. But if we take on or agree with that fear, we have entered into it and it becomes the evil that defiles us. Even Jesus was tempted, but "sinned not."[34] In contrast, the devil and his workers also have the ability to speak to our mind (soul) through our spirit because he is in the spiritual realm.

For the ***word of God*** *is quick, and powerful, and sharper than any twoedged sword, piercing even to the dividing asunder of soul and spirit, and of the joints and marrow, and* ***is a discerner of the thoughts and intents of the heart****. (Hebrews 4:12)* We need to be discerners. But we can only discern by being sensitive to the Holy Spirit in the knowledge of the Word and character of God.

Words speak to our spirit and soul. If they speak to our spirit and they are in alignment with our soul (mind), then the words become one within us. Therefore, we become one in agreement with the Word of God when our soul and spirit agree. If a thought that doesn't match up with the Word, comes through the spirit of man, we can cast it down for what it is – a thought or imagination that is against the Word of God. *Casting down imaginations, and every high thing that exalteth itself against*

---

[34] Hebrews 4:15 *For we have not an high priest which cannot be touched with the feeling of our infirmities; but was in all points tempted like as we are, yet without sin.*

the knowledge of God, and bringing into captivity every thought to the obedience of Christ; (2 Corinthians 10:5)

The Unloving Spirit

Many times stress and anxiety is coupled with an unloving spirit. To be free of fear, we must be able to receive God's love and feel safe in it regardless if anybody else loves us or not. That's part of the relationship with God that we must have – love and trust.

If we are waiting for our family and everyone to make us feel loved all the time, it is going to be a long, hard road. God is love. God is to be our first love. It is Him from whom we must receive approval and love, not men. David said, *"Create in me a clean heart, O God; and renew* ***a right spirit*** *within me." (Psalms 51:10)* It is each one of us, not another person, who has to get right and escape the bonds of the enemy first. We can't expect or wait on another before getting a right spirit within ourselves.

We must resolve that God placed us here, in this generation and loves us beyond measure. *There is no fear in love; but perfect love casteth out fear: because fear hath torment. He that feareth is not made perfect in love. (1 John 4:18)* We have to believe the Word of God, and that He knew and loved us before we were born. *My frame was not hidden from you when I was made in the secret place. When I was woven together in the depths of the earth, your eyes saw my unformed body. All the days ordained for me were written in your book before one of them came to be. (Psalms 139:15, 16 NIV)*

Fear and the lack of love, or the knowledge of His love, go hand in hand. If we know we are loved, what goes? – Fear.

As often happens, God brought this fact home to me under some extremely trying circumstances one evening when I attempted to remove a tree from our backyard. Instead of this 100+ foot behemoth falling the way I thought it should, it began falling toward our house! However, it got hung up in a giant beech tree that inhibited its fall with one tiny limb! As darkness came I was faced with this giant tree, off and free of its trunk, leaning precariously toward my home. I moved my visiting daughter and grandchildren to the other end of the house and tried to pray my way through the great fear that kept coming upon me.

While I was able to put down the fear temporarily, it continued to plague my sleep. I wouldn't slumber very long until fear would engulf me once again. Then, finally about 3:30AM my wife received the word of the Lord and said to me, "Randy, why are you in fear? You know God loves you." Those words struck my spirit and calmed my soul because God's supernatural expression of love for me is the anchor that gave strength to answer the call to ministry and a walk of faith. Above all else, I know God loves me and works things to my good as the scripture says.[35] So, whether the tree came through the house or not, it would be for my ultimate good. I went back to bed and slept soundly.

However, fear made one last attempt to grab me as I awoke to an increasing wind that was blowing toward the house. Yet, I did not fear and was able to rest in God's love and his protection because I know above all else, that my Father loves

[35] Romans 8:28, 29 *And we know that all things work together for good to them that love God, to them who are the called according to his purpose. For whom he did foreknow, he also did predestinate to be conformed to the image of his Son, that he might be the firstborn among many brethren.*

me. (God provided some professional emergency tree removers so that the tree did not fall into the house.)

Again, if there is no fear in love and we have God's love, then what has to go? Fear has to go. 1 John 4:18 says *perfect love casteth out fear.* We must make a decision to walk in love for God and man and **be** love. Receive God's love. His love through one man, Jesus Christ, sanctified the world forever. Listen to the Good Shepherd. He that knows the voice of the shepherd, another voice he will not follow.[36]

Fruits of Fear

We are to be fearless and have no "hooks" in us that the devil can use to direct our lives. Only then will the fruits of fear not be manifested in our lives.

In 1997 the Associated Press ran a story stating that John Hopkins medical research indicated that asthma is a result of fears, stress and anxiety. Yes, there are mutant genes that can be passed down the generations and make you much more susceptible, but fear is still the culprit for its manifestation and hold.

When we allow fear to control us, sorrow comes with it. (Fear hath torment.) We wonder why we have lost our joy for and in living! When we begin to conquer our fears, joy and the joy of spirit will be returned like a fresh drink of water. In other words when we are washed by the water of the Word, there is refreshment and joy to our soul and to others around us.

---

[36] John 10:5

As we've said before, both faith and fear demands a response. One could just as easily say, "According to your fear so be it unto you." *For the thing which I greatly feared is come upon me, and that which I was afraid of* ***is come unto me****. (Job 3:25)* What Job feared came upon him. We need to stand in belief and ask Father, that according to my faith be it unto me. You that have fear say, "Father I'm sorry for following my fears because they demand to be fulfilled. I ask for your mercy to change me and my thinking."

When Jesus was faced with fear all around him what did he do? He rebuked the wind and said unto the sea, "peace, be still." (Mark 4:39) Just as faith is the opposite of fear so is God's peace the opposite of fear's fruit of torment.

Jesus said, *Peace I leave with you, my peace I give unto you: not as the world giveth, give I unto you. Let not your heart be troubled, neither let it be afraid. (John 14:27)* Now, who are we going to believe? Who are we going to follow? Are we going to follow Jesus or that fear that's trying to grip us?

Jesus' Way

When Jesus was faced with the fear of the storm He **rebuked** the storm and in doing so the power behind the storm. So how do we overcome the storms in our lives that would grip us? We have to **speak** to those storms that would bring us under bondage – just like Jesus did. We are washed by the water of the Word and we need to practice using it. This isn't mind over matter. This is allowing God to build your faith and new long-term physiological memory patterns as you meditate and speak forth the Word of God.

It is a fact that we can break old habits, like being fearful, by forming new habits to replace the old ones. Many believe that if you can break the old and replace them with the new for twenty-eight days, a new mind-body connection will be established. However, we need to replace our habitual thinking patterns with the antidote to our fears and not another poor substitute. Too many people become overweight when they quit smoking and substitute the habit of reaching into the refrigerator to satisfy the old nicotine desire of their body.

How is a habit developed? Habits are established by repetition. So why don't we develop new habits of repeatedly believing and using the Word to strengthen our faith and develop new patterns of reaction and thinking? We must repeatedly speak forth the Word when facing the enemy of fear within.

Do you think that Jesus was pushing them into faith when he said to the disciples, ***Why are ye so fearful*[37]*? How is it that ye have no faith? (Mark 4:40 KJV)***

OUCH!! What is he saying? He is saying that fear is the opposite of faith.

Do we now understand why fear is disobedience to God? Is there understanding that fear is a sin? Fear is definitely sin. Did not Jesus tell us that we would be faced with fears, rejections and sufferings in order to be like him? Yes, and so was he! Just because we will be in the middle of such attacks, doesn't mean fear has to VISIT us in our house (body), which is the temple of God. Do we now understand why we have to confess and ask forgiveness for accepting our fears? They are sin. Then we can be delivered and walk out to freedom with a new game plan in our head. This is a game plan that will bring new, normal reaction in our bodies. We need to be obedient to

[37]Greek: *deilos* from *deo*: dread, by implication faithless – Strongs 1169

God's commands, "FEAR NOT." Being able to obey this command through a love relationship with, and trust in, the Lord may soon be the difference between the abundant life in Christ or death. *And there shall be signs in the sun, and in the moon, and in the stars; and upon the earth distress of nations, with perplexity; the sea and the waves roaring; Men's hearts failing them for fear, and for looking after those things which are coming on the earth: for the powers of heaven shall be shaken. (Luke 21:25, 26)*

Fear and Relationships With Others

There are two kingdoms and two dimensions operating in the earth – God's and Satan's; physical and spiritual. Just as we see each other, so do the spirits in the invisible (to us) kingdom see each other. Complementary and/or supporting spirits, generically called "coupling spirits" are attracted to each other to perpetuate Satan's kingdom. Complementary spirits are those who need each other to be complete in function. Supporting spirits are those whose position is reinforced or solidified by the other.

The scriptures show us several relationship examples of this manifestation. One of the best case studies is the relationship between King Ahab and Jezebel as recorded in the 18th chapter of 1 Kings. While their relationship and the study of their coupling characteristics could be the subject for a book in and of itself, let me attempt to explain in a most simplistic analysis.

Ahab, who God called more wicked than all the kings before him, was intrinsically a weak and submissive personality who needed someone he could trust to lead him and control/manipulate his domain in order to achieve his desires. His weakness and fears of being conquered were initially demonstrated in his mutual defense contract marriage to the foreigner, Jezebel, daughter of Ethbaal, king of Sidon. In contrast, Jezebel was a strong, controlling, dominant personality.

In this relationship, Ahab's weaknesses and fears needed the completion or complementary characteristics in Jezebel's dominance and leadership. In contrast, Jezebel needed to dominate and rule. In order for her to be fulfilled she needed a conduit like Ahab. The weak needed the strong and the strong needed the weak.

Unfortunately, we observe these same attractions occurring repeatedly to destroy the lives and testimony of Christian men and women. For example, a spiritually wounded Christian woman who has been dominated by her father in childhood is particularly vulnerable to these spirits. "Something" in her is often unconsciously seeking a dominant marriage partner to fulfill her association between dominance and the security of a strong provider. So when a dominating unsaved man shows her love (one of mankind's strongest emotions), she perceives security. Her fear of being unloved will block out remembering the intensity of distress that came with being dominated. On the other side, "something" in an unsaved man wants not only to possess her, but also to dominate and victimize her. Why? The "something" within them are spirits working together to destroy God's rulership in both their lives and further the kingdom of Satan. That is why people tend to enter into relationship with, or even marry, the same kind of person again and again.

<u>Fear drives us into relationships</u>. Generally, this is because of our need to be loved. Situational victimization, or one time occurrences, that try to bring on fear can happen. However, continual victimization has to be dealt with. Until a person really deals with their sin, we must withdraw from those who

continually "repent" of victimization, abuse, etc., but never really evidence change. A repetitive abuser of women, for example, will abuse again until it is dealt with on a spiritual level.

In regard to relationships with others, let me point out that perfectionism and control are similar in this realm of the spirit. As a matter of fact perfectionism is a form of control. There is a spirit of fear behind them that says my future is in my own hands. If I have all knowledge of all things and can move all the pieces around in my eyesight, then my destiny is in my own hands. However, the avoidance of this fear of the future, through perfectionism, can be devastating to the ones we love.

Perfectionism has caused more fear **spirits to enter into children** than can be imagined. Our society is based on success. God's "society" is based on victories that begin in failure and reliance/trust upon Him. Man's society makes no allowance for failure. In contrast, God says in your weakness, I will make you strong. Man and man's values have given us fear because it says that our worth is based on success and perfection.

I'd like to make one last brief point on the subject of interpersonal relationships. If somebody gets in our face and we have distressing feelings of anguish about it several days later, then we have something to deal with – the thing that set us off. It was very possibly an unloving spirit plus fear, rejection, pride, abandonment, etc.

Examples: Fear and Consequences Named

The fruits of fear are all the physiological consequences of long term fear. This includes such illnesses as heart conditions, mitro valve prolapse, irritable bowel syndrome, mal-absorption, asthma, reflux, frigidity, impotence, Graves, acid reflux disease, etc. All these and many others are rooted in fear.

Fear of Dreams; *In thoughts from the visions of the night, when deep sleep falleth on men, Fear came upon me, and trembling, which made all my bones to shake. Then a spirit passed before my face; the hair of my flesh stood up: (Job 4:13-16)*

Often the doorway to fearful "visions of the night" is a horror movie that gives rise to nightmares and terror of the night. In order to be free of these night terrors, we are going to have to recognize our sin and repent of every childhood horror flick we've ever watched as the Lord will bring them to our mind. Additionally, we must be careful what we see as an adult – especially before going to sleep. When we are at rest our conscious guard is down, and we are more susceptible to hearing the spiritual kingdoms.

Even God will use our slumber to bypass our pride in order to save us from our path of destruction: *For God speaketh once, yea twice, yet man perceiveth it not. In a dream, in a vision of the night, when deep sleep falleth upon men, in slumberings upon the bed; Then he openeth the ears of men, and sealeth their instruction, That he may withdraw man from his purpose, and hide pride from man. He keepeth back his soul from the pit, and his life from perishing by the sword. (Job 33:14-18)*

God tells us that we must be careful what we see as the last of six evidences of who will stand in the burnings of His testings: *Hear, ye that are far off, what I have done; and, ye that are near, acknowledge my might. The sinners in Zion* (Church) *are afraid; <u>fearfulness</u> hath surprised the hypocrites. Who among us shall dwell with the devouring fire?* (God's judging fire) *who among us shall dwell with everlasting burnings?* (Who can stand it?) *He that 1. walketh righteously, and 2. speaketh uprightly* (watch your words); *3. he that despiseth the gain of oppressions, 4. that shaketh his hands from holding of bribes, 5. that stoppeth his ears from hearing of blood* (plots of murder), *and 6.* ***shutteth his eyes from seeing evil.*** (WE NEED TO BE CAREFUL OF THE MOVIES, BOOKS, VIDEO GAMES, INTERNET SITES, AND MAGAZINES, THAT WE, AND OUR FAMILY, LOOK AT!) *He shall dwell on high: his place of defence shall be the munitions of rocks: bread shall be given him; his waters shall be sure. Thine eyes shall see the king in his beauty: they shall behold the land that is very far off. (Isaiah 33:13-17)*

Several years ago I was given a first hand experience of the principle of keeping our eyes from seeing evil. About a week after I had received a life changing encounter with the Holy Spirit, my wife and I were on an airplane ride to California for a business meeting. At the time, I continued to walk in a state of constant anointing from the powerful infilling of the Holy Spirit that I had received the week before.

I was studying the scriptures and being greatly edified when the attendant announced that they were offering a movie on the flight entitled, "Clear and Present Danger" staring Harrison Ford. Since I was an ardent Tom Clancy fan and had read this book, I had been expectantly awaiting the release of the movie. However, something in my spirit said not to rent the earphones. So I didn't. Yet, when the movie came on the overhead screens I found myself sneaking peeks – right up to the opening ambush of the car caravan. I looked to see one explosion and death after another. Each time my spirit and body would wrench in anguish. Though I would look away my brain couldn't quite accept the "coincidence" of the "pain" that was happening in my body. So I'd look back again, just to again be whapped with strong revulsion and anguish. God was teaching me that this was no coincidence!

In walking out our freedom it is extremely important to be aware what we take in. Even casual entertainment, will impact our thinking and memory. We must try to remain sensitive to the Spirit's cautions. Let us understand that the Lord was trying to teach us another kingdom principle when he told us: *Be ye angry, and sin not: let not the sun go down upon your wrath:* (Eph 4:26) When we go to sleep with impressions or thoughts that evoke negative feelings, we are allowing that record to go round and round in our subconscious.

I recently went to bed immediately after watching a rather heart rending television rerun episode of "Third Watch" in which a child was abducted. Although the storyline resulted in a happy ending of the child being found, I was disturbed by the trauma and generated anxiety of the search and fight with the abductor. I awoke the next morning thinking about, and still feeling, the violence that I had seen.

I was reminded that when I was overcoming fear, I absolutely had to go to sleep with either worship music or the Word of God on the stereo. It was the only way I could get enough peace to get any rest at all.

We need to guard our heart[38] and our eyes – even from the news, if it is drawing us. If we are abiding in Him and remain objective while watching the news on television, we're probably all right. However, if we haven't overcome our fears and learned to trust Him for our peace, then we must realize that the

[38] Proverbs 4:23 *Keep thy heart with all diligence; for out of it are the issues of life.*

news' media agenda is to grab us with the spectacular. In doing so, they transmit fear and bad events with 95% of their coverage. If we are not careful, the repeated exposure can bring fear and depression because of the world's events.

The Promise of God for our Obedience:

My son, let not them (GOD'S PRECEPTS) *depart from thine eyes: keep sound wisdom and discretion: So shall they be life unto thy soul, and grace to thy neck. Then shalt thou walk in thy way safely, and thy foot shall not stumble.* ***When thou liest down, thou shalt not be afraid: yea, thou shalt lie down, and thy sleep shall be sweet.*** *(Proverbs 3:21-24)*

If ye walk in my statutes, and keep my commandments, and do them;... (Leviticus 26:3) And I will give peace in the land, and ye shall lie down, and none shall make you afraid: and I will rid evil beasts out of the land, neither shall the sword go through your land. (Leviticus 26:6) But whoso hearkeneth unto me shall dwell safely, and shall be quiet from fear of evil. (Proverbs 1:33)

A Psalm of David. The LORD is my light and my salvation; whom shall I fear? The LORD is the strength of my life; of whom shall I be afraid? When the wicked, even mine enemies and my foes, came upon me to eat up my flesh, they stumbled and fell. Though an host should encamp against me, my heart shall not fear: though war should rise against me, in this will I be confident. (Psalms 27:1-3)

Chapter 7
Summary

1. Our words demand response and fulfillment.

2. Our words can bring us justification and life or condemnation and death.

3. In order to be loosed from fear, we must be able to receive the perfect love of God. (Perfect love casts out fear.)

4. God abhors us to watch evil. If we do watch evil, we will be susceptible to tormenting "visions of the night."

5. Obedience to Gods commands will grant us "sweet sleep," without fear.

Chapter Eight

Review

Fear is the corruption of the normal fight or flight mechanism that God built into our make up. At some point, either through generational inheritance or by our own acceptance of an evil spirit, fear has entered in to impress a chemical reaction in our body causing the long term memories to generate fear responses.

We are all the product of the curse[39]. If mankind had not sinned we would not have to worry about disease because there would be none. Deuteronomy 28 says disease is caused by sin (or sometimes tragedy). This sin can be either generational or personal sins.

The Lamb of God so loved His church that He gave His life to sanctify and make us clean through the life that is in His Word: *...Christ also loved the church, and gave himself for it; that he might sanctify and cleanse it with the washing of water by the word,.. (Ephesians 5:25, 26)* This is an on going process of believing and apprehending (i.e. faith) His gift for our sanctification and cleansing. Jesus taught us that to think evil "in our heart" is just as much a sin as to do evil. (Matthew 5:28) Yet, without even realizing that evil thoughts are sin, the body of Christ continues in our deception and contemplates upon all manner of lust, slander, jealousy, judgments, fears, etc. Unless

[39] See page 16

we begin to discern, repent and ask God's forgiveness, we will suffer the spiritual and physical consequences. We must quit drinking from the polluted waters of man's rationalized thinking and begin drinking from the clean, pure water of life – every Word coming forth from the mouth of God.

This washing by the Word means that we must change our way of thinking to align with the Word of God. We must repent and undergo an attitude adjustment. A double minded man has one part of his mind in the kingdom of God and another in the kingdom of Satan. He is unstable in all his ways. We have to embrace only the kingdom of God and a way of thinking that only aligns with the Word of God. Whatever is not of faith that we allow to stay with us, will be the rotten apple that spoils the whole bushel. One opening invites supportive spirits of fear.

DEEDS OF THE FLESH

What do the scriptures call the deeds of the flesh? *Now the* ***works of the flesh*** *are manifest, which are these; Adultery, fornication, uncleanness, lasciviousness, Idolatry, witchcraft, hatred, variance* (CONTENTION), *emulations* (JEALOUSY), *wrath* (FITS OF RAGE), *strife, seditions* (DISUNION), *heresies, envyings, murders, drunkenness, revellings, and such like: of the which I tell you before, as I have also told you in time past, that they which do such things shall not inherit the kingdom of God. (Galatians 5:19-21)* The "works of the flesh" are not "flesh" as in the meat, skin and bones, but they are "flesh" because they come out of the body. The "works of the flesh" are spirits within that manifest their influence over the body to give obedience to the kingdom of darkness.

For if ye live after the flesh (the sin that dwells within you), *ye shall die* (physically and spiritually): *but if ye <u>through the Spirit</u>*

do mortify (kill) *the deeds of the body* (The manifested "deeds" of the body are of the devil.), *ye shall live. For as many as are led by the Spirit of God, they are the sons of God. For ye have not received the* ***spirit of bondage*** (Hebrews 2:15 says that is the fear of death.) *again to fear; but ye have received the Spirit of adoption, whereby we cry, Abba, Father. (Romans 8:13-15)* Fear is bondage. Let me say it again. Fear is bondage!

The "need to know" everything is driven by fear, divination and witchcraft. The "need to know" is rooted in fears. Specifically in regard to fears, the fear of tomorrow and the fear of loss drives the "need to know." Dread is a projection of evil into the future. In other words, it is an expectation that something will go wrong. By knowing everything, the individual hopes to control or avoid potentially adverse situations and minimize their dread of tomorrow.

The Bible says: *Take therefore no thought for the morrow: for the morrow shall take thought for the things of itself. Sufficient unto the day is the evil thereof. (Matthew 6:34)* We are supposed to take no thought of tomorrow by worrying about what the future may bring. However, some of us are so busy reflecting on the evil of the past and projecting it into tomorrow, we have neglected to take care of the fear and evil of today. Some spend their life projecting their fears into their possible future.

Fear also causes a form of blindness. It clouds our memory, confuses our thinking and obscures our faith.

During my personal battle to overcome fear the tasks that used to be challenging fun became nearly impossible. I had always been able to repair most mechanical and electrical things around the house. As a matter of fact I got a great deal of satisfaction from my ability to "figure things out" and make a repair "as good as new." Then the garage door opener stripped the drive gears and we couldn't lock the door or get out easily. As I climbed the stepladder to dismantle it and investigate the problem, I came to the point of tears and began shaking violently because I feared that I wouldn't remember how to put it back together a week or so later when I could get the part to repair it. I just couldn't remember things or reason.

I felt as disoriented as Nebuchadnezzar must have been when he was driven mad and ate grass (Daniel 4:33). Even every simple task I had to do, from making a phone call to keeping the checkbook, became a monumental obstacle to overcome because I just couldn't think clearly. I would find myself driving down the expressway and suddenly experience the confusing feeling of being lost. Then, more fears and disorientation would come upon me because I didn't recognize where I was. The experience would almost bring me to tears as I tried with everything in me to focus. It wasn't until I would cry out to Jesus and repeatedly speak the Word that my foggy mind would clear enough to realize I had simply not noticed the many familiar landmarks along the way.

Fear caused blindness in Hagar as well: *And God heard the voice of the lad; and the angel of God called to Hagar out of heaven, and said unto her, What aileth thee, Hagar?* ***fear not****; for God hath heard the voice of the lad where he is. Arise, lift up the lad, and hold him in thine hand; for I will make him a great nation. And* ***God opened her eyes****, and she saw a well of water; and she went, and filled the bottle with water, and gave the lad drink. (Genesis 21:17-19)*

It is in this desperation that the Holy Spirit can teach us to totally trust God. We certainly can't trust our own abilities or reasoning any longer. The Word of God is the light and the candle of the Lord. *For thou wilt light my candle: the LORD my God will enlighten my darkness. (Psalms 18:28)* Our heavenly father desires that we recognize and repent of the sinful thoughts that keep us in bondage. We must ask and be willing for Him to show us the depths of deception that reign within our hearts.

We also have to settle the fact that we trust God for our resurrection whether we are physically healed or not. Otherwise we can receive a fear of death/dying and that delivers us into bondage[40]. Did Jesus conquer death, hell and the grave or not? If He did, and we are His children, why should we fear death and going to be with Him? Do we fear death because we leave much undone, including rearing our children and seeing our grandchildren grow up? Then we fear granting God His will in our life - if that is His will. For God, not Satan has the power over life and death. *Forasmuch then as the children are partakers of flesh and blood, he also himself likewise took part of the same; that through death he might destroy him that* ***had*** *the power of death, that is, the devil; And deliver them who* ***through fear of death were all their lifetime subject to bondage.*** *(Hebrews 2:14,15)*

I'm not saying that we shouldn't be wise to preserve the life that God has given us to accomplish His glory in us. I'm saying we should not fear. Going to be with Him as the good and faithful servant should be the goal of our life. We have to believe and know that our life on earth is only a fraction of the life we have with God. So if I die, I live and let God's will be done. We

[40] Hebrews 2:15

must quit trying to preserve our life – or we'll lose it.[41] Trust in God.

What the devil plans against us for evil, God will use for our good so "fear not." *And Joseph said unto them, Fear not: for am I in the place of God? But as for you, ye thought evil against me; but God meant it unto good, to bring to pass, as it is this day, to save much people alive. Now therefore fear ye not: I will nourish you, and your little ones. And he comforted them, and spake kindly unto them. (Genesis 50:19-21)* During my most desperate times of fear the one scripture that I believed and grabbed on to with all that I had was: *And we know that all things work together for good to them that love God, to them who are the called according to his purpose. For whom he did foreknow, he also did predestinate to be conformed to the image of his Son, that he might be the firstborn among many brethren. (Romans 8:28,29)*

Unless we continuously come to repentance, hear, and obey what the Spirit is saying, fear will be the ship to take us back into bondage. Do you remember the teaching on Deuteronomy 28:68?[42] *And the LORD shall bring thee into Egypt again with ships, by the way whereof I spake unto thee, Thou shalt see it no more again: and there ye shall be sold unto your enemies for bondmen and bondwomen, and no man shall buy you. (Deuteronomy 28:68)*

Will fear try to encompass us again? Let's read about the recorded exodus: *And when Pharaoh drew nigh, the children of Israel lifted up their eyes, and, behold, the Egyptians marched*

---

[41] Matthew 16:25 *For whosoever will save his life shall lose it: and whosoever will lose his life for my sake shall find it.*

[42] See page 68

after them; and they were <u>*sore afraid*</u>*: and the children of Israel cried out unto the LORD. And they said unto Moses, Because there were no graves in Egypt, hast thou taken us away to die in the wilderness? wherefore hast thou dealt thus with us, to carry us forth out of Egypt? (Exodus 14:10,11)* They began to disbelieve God because of fear – they were "sore afraid." Fear, generated by our own disobedience, will take us right back into bondage again.

Today, many people are just like the Israelites. They do not want to recognize and be delivered from their fears either. Deliverance from fear demands that we give up our own will unto the Lord's and overcome through battle. Many in the Body of Christ have been deceived, and will confess that their fears are "just who I am." Such a response jumped off the screen a few years back when I saw a Star Trek movie entitled, "Undiscovered Country." In this movie the Vulcan brother of Commander Spock commandeered the Starship Enterprise in his quest to find a mythical "Shaka'ree," the supposed dwelling place of God. Spock's brother had the ability to relieve fear and its resulting pain. However, Captain Kirk rejected the offer for freedom from his past and responded with the same lie as many Christians hold by saying, "I need my fears. That's who I am."

Fears are not who you are and are not to be the driving inspiration for your life or your work. If you are in fear of your boss in the workplace, and that fear of man is the driving force behind your performance, then you are setting yourself up for all kinds of physical maladies. Our bodies are simply not designed to sustain the high chemical output that fear brings. Fear will drive you into sickness and bondage. Even the Israelites did not want to be delivered when the fear of death came upon them. They willed to go back into Egypt and the familiarity, "security" and torment of their slavery. We may think, "Oh how foolish they were." But many of us make the same choice today. In order to be the person we were created to be, we must receive the Lord's will and take up the battle for our freedom.

Our normal, God given fear response is built into us as a fight or flight mechanism that allows decision. We have a decision to make. When we decide to flee, our body should return to normal after the danger passes. However, if we stay in a flight mode, our backside is uncovered by the armor of God. Once we have accepted Satan's fears in the "wells" of our soul, they push away the Holy Spirit's guidance and substitute the enemies' promptings. Unfortunately, the more we embrace the enemy's fear the more slow we are to seek the Holy Spirit and return to do battle. We become deceived because this is now an area that we have given to the enemy. The Holy Spirit doesn't usually return to give us freedom without our seeking Him, but rather he returns to face the enemy with us. We may be facing the demons in faith, but we may also be facing them with fear. It is imperative for us to "stand" in faith and let the Lord fight our battle.

Now here's the problem. We, as a physical and spiritual creation are being terrorized by invisible beings and have to rely upon an invisible helper. Isn't it amazing that we will often listen to the invisible enemy more than we listen to our invisible helper? Fear is designed to steal our faith AND our life. If Satan can't keep us from being saved, he'll try to make us an ineffective Christian through our fears. However, God says, that we are not to fear because He will never leave or forsake us. (Hebrews 13:5)

Sometimes people don't receive truth because they have no knowledge. If we take flight and stay alarmed even after the danger is over, then we are programmed to run. If we become programmed to run, the enemy will run over us. In contrast, if we have understanding through the Word we've heard and been taught, we'll be able to better understand and stand in faith. Fear will try to get us to forget what God did for us yesterday so that he can overcome us today and tomorrow. That's one reason why the Israelites were always reminding themselves of the many miracles God did for them. We should too. We have to keep reminding ourselves of how good God has been to us and remember that His mercy endures forever.

Faith leads, *(For as many as are led by the Spirit of God, are the sons of God. – Romans 8:14)*
Fear drives. *(Behold, I will bring a fear upon thee, saith the Lord GOD of hosts, from all those that be about thee; and ye shall be driven out every man right forth; and none shall gather up him that wandereth. – Jeremiah 49:5)*

Chapter 8
Summary

1. Fear is the corruption of the normal fight or flight mechanisms God gave us.

2. "Works of the flesh" are spirits within that manifest their control over the body to give obedience to the kingdom of darkness.

3. Fear will blind us and give us wrong or obscured thinking.

4. Ruling fears, which are the opposite of faith, will lead us back into the bondage of Egypt - the world's ways.

5. Freedom from fear demands that you give up your own will unto the Lord's and overcome through battle.

Chapter Nine

Overcoming Fear

Up to this point I've tried to illuminate the darkness by sharing God's Word and my personal experiences regarding fears. Let's reexamine fear's:

1. Character – it is a spirit. *For God hath not given us the spirit of fear; but of power, and of love, and of a sound mind (2 Timothy 1:7)*

2. Origin – fear enters through sin. *I also will choose their delusions, and will bring their fears upon them; because when I called, none did answer; when I spake, they did not hear: (Isaiah 66:4)*

3. Destruction of faith. *Whatsoever is not of faith is sin. (Romans 14:23)*

4. Effects on our bodies – sickness. *Wherefore it shall come to pass, if ye hearken to these judgments, and keep, and do them, that the LORD thy God shall keep unto thee the covenant and the mercy which he sware unto thy fathers:.. And the LORD will take away from thee all sickness, and will put none of the evil diseases of Egypt, which thou knowest, upon thee; but will lay them upon all them that hate thee. (Deuteronomy 7:12,15)*

5. Antidote – the Word of God. *For the word of God is quick, and powerful, and sharper than any twoedged*

sword, piercing even to the dividing asunder of soul and spirit, and of the joints and marrow, and is a discerner of the thoughts and intents of the heart. (Hebrews 4:12)

The Lord has said time and time again, that without knowledge **His people:**

1. Go into captivity - *Therefore my people are gone into captivity, because they have no knowledge: and their honourable men are famished, and their multitude dried up with thirst. (Isaiah 5:13-14)*

2. Become separated from God - *"…because thou hast rejected knowledge, I will also reject thee, that thou shalt be no priest to me: seeing thou hast forgotten the law of thy God, I will also forget thy children." (Hosea 4:6)*

3. Are destroyed - *My people are destroyed for lack of knowledge: (Hosea 4:6)*

But now His Word has given us knowledge: *For God, who commanded the light to shine out of darkness, hath shined in our hearts, to give the light of the knowledge of the glory of God in the face of Jesus Christ. (2 Corinthians 4:6)* With this knowledge and understanding it is time for us to break the bonds upon ourselves first and then others. We must apprehend or appropriate this Word and the promises of God to deliver us from the bondage which has kept us ensnared from moving higher in His commission and calling for our lives.

We can not afford to delay and just avoid our fears. To do so is sin that can lead to disease and death. We need to recognize and detest the fears within us and begin our quest, yes our war, for freedom. Each one of us needs to deal with them at their very root. If we don't deal with them, not only will we be stagnant and dying in our spiritual walk toward righteousness and obedience, we might very well be one of those whose heart will fail at the circumstances which will accompany the coming of our Lord and Savior, Jesus Christ.[43]

As believers in Jesus Christ we have been called to war against the spiritual realm of darkness ruled by Satan. This war begins in your own land – the temple of God that is your body. Each one of us must wrestle with the evil thoughts that raise themselves up against God's Word. If we do not battle by *casting down imaginations, and every high thing that exalteth itself against the knowledge of God, and bringing into captivity every thought to the obedience of Christ; (2 Corinthians 10:5),* then we give ourselves over to thinking patterns that establish Satan's rule, or a "throne," in our life. These thrones are positions of power in our thought processes that establish whose kingdom authority will rule over our life – Satan's or God's.

People try to deal with their fears every day through the knowledge of the world. They go to psychologists, psychiatrists and doctors for help. Many consume pills for the rest of their lives to help mask some of the symptoms of fear, but never deal with the root cause. With the root problem intact and associated spirits still manipulating their body, the pills become blockers to normal sensory functioning. Their body continues to produce increasing hormones and there will continue to be the resulting sickness/infirmities and even death over time.

---

[43] Luke 21:26 *Men's hearts failing them for fear, and for looking after those things which are coming on the earth: for the powers of heaven shall be shaken.*

Nearly everyone who has been on anti-depressant drugs will tell you that the drugs only allow you to cope with life, but not live fully. While they bring some sanity back to a tormented mind, the fear is constantly trying to break through, bypassing the blocking medicine. We then experience twinges of fear, and become consumed with rationalizing and controlling our emotions instead of walking in the peace that Jesus left with us.

In these last days before Christ's return, God is judging and challenging His people to expose the root of fear and overcome it, so it doesn't overcome us. In order to become like Christ, we must tear down the ruling thrones and thinking patterns that Satan has established within us. We have a choice to accept our Creator's diagnosis of fear and faithfully accept His medicine (the Word of God), or be tormented until our hearts fail us. The choice is up to each one of us.

The list at the end of this book contains many fears common to man. Do you identify with any of them? Or are there others not mentioned that plague your life? If you do, I would like to encourage you because God wants to begin setting you free. In order to get free of those bonds you need to recognize that those tormenting spirits of fear are not the real you and they are not of God. God has not given the spirit of fear to you! Fears are the enemies of your soul who are intent on your destruction.

You do not have to live with them. The first thing you must do after identifying fears in your life is to take responsibility for your part in accepting them into your life. This may sound simple, but while many people will acknowledge their fears, they want to put the blame for them on circumstances, other people or traumatic situations. Deep down, in the recesses of their being they blame God, others, or accidents. Some simply can't get beyond Satan's thrones of self pity, pride or other blockages to take responsibility for their part in receiving the spirits of fear that torment them. As a result, complete freedom from fears is impossible until God reveals and deals with the blockages.

I once ministered to an anointed young mother I shall call Sheila (not her real name). Sheila truly desired to walk the narrow path of righteousness and obedience to God's Word. She also was ministering under the anointing power of the Holy Spirit.

However, during her youth Sheila had become plagued with fears. Her family moved at the beginning of her sophomore year of high school. This transition was difficult for Sheila as she had a hard time finding friends and "fitting in." The rest of her teenage years evidenced rebellion to God, parents, and nearly all authority. She "hung" with kids of questionable character and different religious beliefs. She attended a two-year Christian college only to continue in her ways.

By the time she graduated from a state college she had repented and turned her life to God. After resisting the devil for nearly a year, God mercifully granted her significant deliverance just before she married. However, she remained very self oriented and carried many fears including a belief that God would punish her former sins and lifestyle by not allowing her to bear children. The prophetic word came to rebuke that lie of Satan two years before the birth of her first child. When the baby was born she suffered with what the medical profession calls post partum syndrome. She became depressed and so obsessed with fears that she couldn't enjoy the blessing of the new life that God had given her to nurture.

As she began to walk out her salvation in trusting God and calling upon His Word according to the principles contained in this book, she made significant progress. However, she would only remain victorious for short periods of time until fear came to grip her again. She continued to struggle with fear until God revealed the reasons through a word of knowledge. In her torment she had cried out for relief and asked forgiveness for her unbelief in taking fear upon herself. However, she continued to blame and harbor ill feelings toward her parents for moving the family residence during her high school years!

Jesus taught us: *For if ye forgive men their trespasses, your heavenly Father will also forgive you: (Matthew 6:14)* While this well known scripture pretty well covers unforgiveness, what does the Word say about blaming other's? *Then you will call, and **the LORD will answer**; you will cry for help, and he will say: Here am I. "**If you do away with** the yoke of oppression, with **the pointing finger** and malicious talk, (Isaiah 58:9 NIV)* When will the Lord answer our cry for help? He'll answer when we put away blaming others for our own sin. In spite of her remorse, Sheila's lack of forgiveness and "pointing finger" of blame were the very sins that blocked her own restoration! By holding on to these thrones of Satan, the lying thoughts prevented her from taking sole responsibility for her own sinful actions. Once she cried out and took responsibility for her acceptance of the enemies' entrapments, the Lord could work toward her deliverance, restoration and stability.

Just like Sheila, many people are sorry for their sins because they are under the torment of the oppressors they've enthroned. They have no concept of their sin because they can only look at it from their own selfish perspective of how they have hurt themselves or from an academic understanding of the Word that it is sin. However, until we start perceiving sin from God's perspective, we haven't moved into a relationship framed by the intimacy of love that He is calling us to. Oh, how our sin hurts the heart of God, our Elohim, our Lord, Savior, lover and husband.

Most of us can identify with the heart-wrenching of being betrayed or "dumped" by a lover, marriage partner, a family member, disciple or anyone else whom we've reached out our heart for. And yet, because God is God, Who loves us beyond measure, we don't attribute the same anguish to Him, when He sees His very own children turn away in disobedience from his instructions. And yet His Spirit is grieved when we do: *And grieve not the Holy Spirit of God, whereby ye are sealed unto the day of redemption. (Ephesians 4:30)*

In speaking to the churches in the book of Revelation, Jesus begins in chapter two by addressing the born again believers in the church of Ephesus:

I know thy works, and thy labour, and thy patience, and how thou canst not bear them which are evil: and thou hast tried them which say they are apostles, and are not, and hast found them liars: And hast borne, and hast patience, and for my name's sake hast laboured, and hast not fainted. Nevertheless I have somewhat against thee, because thou hast left thy first love. Remember therefore from whence thou art fallen, and ***repent****, and do the first works; or else I will come unto thee quickly, and will remove thy candlestick out of his place,* ***except thou repent****. But this thou hast, that thou hatest the deeds of the Nicolaitanes, which I also hate. He that hath an ear, let him hear what the Spirit saith unto the churches; To him that overcometh will I give to eat of the tree of life, which is in the midst of the paradise of God. (Revelation 2:2-7)*

These are Christ's faithful followers who have labored patiently, hate evil, tested the false apostles, not fainted for His Name's sake, and hate the doctrine of the Nicolaitans, as He does also. In spite of these attributes, Jesus says that they must repent of losing their "first love" or face the removal of their candlestick from the Tree of Life and presence of the Lord. The first thing that we need to notice is that Jesus is calling for repentance from His own sheep. This is the next step in our quest to overcome the enemy that besieges us. But what is Jesus telling them to repent from losing?

Many in the Western church would teach you that the "first love" that was lost, is the love of Jesus himself. While this interpretation may preach well, it is not consistent within the context of the passage. It is inconsistent to have lost the love of the Lord and still oppose evil ones, labor patiently and not faint for his name's sake. So again what is the "first love" Jesus is talking about?

I suggest that the Messianic Jewish teachers are correct in their affirmation that our "first love" is His Word, commandments (they would say Torah), instructions, and laws. The gospel of John begins by telling us that Jesus is the Word. Thus we may have an emotional love for our Savior, but if we are not listening, studying, and passionately seeking His Word; that is His commandments (and promises), we have lost our "first love." This is the very Word that first brought us unto the belief, confession and the walk of our salvation! Jesus said, *If ye love me, keep my commandments. (John 14:15)* If he is the Word, then are not His commandments the whole Word – both Old and New Testaments? If we don't come into agreement with and follow the entire Word of God as revealed by the Holy Spirit, we have a serious problem because we will have grieved the Holy Spirit and our Savior will say He has "somewhat against" us.

In Matthew 15:6, Jesus admonished the scribes and Pharisees by telling them that the prophet Elias (Elijah) was right about them when he said that they "made the commandment of God of none effect" by their traditions. And then Jesus said something very pertinent to the discussion of the Ephesus church's "first love," ***But in vain*** *they do worship me, teaching for doctrines the commandments of men. (Matthew 15:9)* Do you realize that our worship is in vain if we do not obey His commandments? So then, let us do as He has commanded and ask forgiveness with a right heart and **repent** for disobeying His commands and accepting the fears that torment us.

Realize that there is not only the feeling, but also a change in both attitude and action required to repent. Let us look at the dictionary again and we'll understand that true repentance is all three definitions:

Webster's dictionary defines "repent" as:

- to **feel** sorry or self-reproachful for what one has done, or failed to do; be conscience-stricken or contrite:

- to feel such regret or dissatisfaction over some past action, intention, etc. as to **change one's mind** about:

- to feel so contrite over one's sins as to change, or decide to **change, one's ways**; be penitent

According to this definition repentance is first of all a **feeling** of sorrow, self reproach, regret and contrition because of our action (or lack of action). Secondly repentance is **a change** of **mind** (thoughts) and "**one's ways**" (actions). If we can get to this stage and begin to obey God, then what does His Word promise? *Wherefore he saith, God resisteth the proud, but giveth grace unto the humble. Submit* (obey) *yourselves therefore to God. Resist the devil, and he will flee from you. (James 4:6,7)* Thus with Godly sorrow and humility we must repent to God and change our thinking and actions to stand in faith on the Word of God.

The next step to freedom is declaring our desires and intent to come out of agreement with the fears. At this point many are trapped by reluctance to go beyond their rational "civility." Our thinking will often allow us to:

- receive knowledge,
- recognize our sin,
- take responsibility and
- repent to God,

because these can be very private actions of the heart. But now I'm suggesting that we speak forth and renounce the spirits of fear that bind us. In chapter 7, we talked about the importance of our words. In the spiritual dimension of the Kingdom of God and even in Satan's kingdom of evil, our words are powerful. They are powerful for both blessing and cursing of ourselves, others and the spirits that besiege us. The Word says, *For with the heart man believeth unto righteousness; and with the mouth confession is made unto salvation. (Romans 10:10)* As we've taught previously, "salvation" is more than eternal life and walking in the kingdom of God after our physical death. Salvation is walking daily in the kingdom of God and His will. Just as the mouth must declare our belief in Jesus, we need to declare our coming out of agreement with the fears that have enthroned themselves in our lives – today!

After we have renounced any agreement with the enemy, the next step is to expel these invaders in our land. What would we do if we discovered the neighborhood ruffians stealing the fruit off our tree and throwing it on the ground? If we didn't want all the fruit wasted, we'd probably be insistent that they remove themselves from our property. We'd insist that they go home and get off our land. If they refused, we might even call the authorities to enforce our property rights.

Likewise we need to expel the (spiritual) enemies from our land (physical bodies and kingdom territory) the same way. The demons of fear have come to steal our spiritual fruit. They have taken our joy and peace and its time we insisted that they get out of our land because Jesus bought back the property rights of our soul, gave us authority and even charged us to tread on them. If they don't want to leave, then we too can appeal to the Lord to send His enforcing authorities, the Holy angels, to evict and escort them to "dry places."

They no longer have a legal right to invade our land because we have repented to God and chosen to come out of agreement with them. In the name of Jesus, we must command these fears to <u>release</u> us from their hold and cut the chains of each one. Just like the invading neighborhood ruffians would be directed to go home, we need to tell the spirits of fear to go back to where they belong – to dry places[44] or where Jesus would send them – and never return again!

Now that you've taken these critical steps, it is time to walk out your freedom in the faith and power of the Word. When the enemy comes at you like a flood, by faith, raise up God's standard – His Word – against those fears. *Resist the devil, and*

[44] Matthew 12:43 *When the unclean spirit is gone out of a man, he walketh through dry places, seeking rest, and findeth none.*

he will flee from you. (James 4:7) Stand fast in faith and resist – take *into captivity every thought to the obedience of Christ; (2 Corinthians 10:5)* As you do this, I am confident that God will bring great restoration to both your spiritual and physical health. *Humble yourselves in the sight of the Lord, and He shall lift you up. (James 4:10)*

Chapter 9
Summary

1. Fear will lead us into captivity, separate us from God and destroy our physical, mental and spiritual well being.

2. With our new-found knowledge of the Word, we can break, and stay free from, the bonds of the enemy.

3. Anti-depressants are a substitute for God's salvation and only provide partial relief from fear.

4. The steps to freedom from fear are:
   - recognition
   - taking responsibility
   - repentance to God
   - renouncing fears
   - expelling fears
   - standing in faith

5. Complete freedom comes when we are delivered from the spirits, our body's RNA secretions return to normal, and our old thought processes have become those of the "new man" in Christ.

Appendix

Aids to Freedom

Practical Steps to Freedom:

1. Make a decision and declare (speak it out) to God that you will come into agreement with His Word and not accept fear anymore.

2. Ask God for a new revelation of His Word that you no longer walk in ignorant disobedience.

3. Ask God for discernment to see more clearly how you are impacted by fear.

4. Repent and ask God to forgive you for each fear that you've given into.

5. Ask God to give you a greater trust (faith) in Him.

6. When fear comes, quote the Word in faith.

7. Associate yourself with a ministry that practices deliverance and can help you to walk in it.

A Psalm of David. The LORD is my light and my salvation; whom shall I fear? the LORD is the strength of my life; of whom shall I be afraid? (Psalms 27:1)

Scriptural Examples Defining Spirits of Fear

Fear of Nothing: ***Psalms 53:5*** *There were they in great fear, where no fear was: for God hath scattered the bones (Heb: 'etsem = bones or substance) of him that encampeth against thee: thou hast put them to shame, because God hath despised them.*

Fear of War: ***Psalms 27:3*** *Though an host should encamp against me, my heart shall not fear: though war should rise against me, in this will I be confident.*

Sudden Fear: ***Proverbs 3:25*** *Be not afraid of sudden fear, neither of the desolation of the wicked, when it cometh.*

Fear of Natural Disaster:
Psalms 46:2,3 *Therefore will not we fear, though the earth be removed, and though the mountains be carried into the midst of the sea; Though the waters thereof roar and be troubled, though the mountains shake with the swelling thereof.*

Matthew 24:6,7 *And ye shall hear of wars and rumours of wars: see that ye be not troubled: for all these things must come to pass, but the end is not yet. For nation shall rise against nation, and kingdom against kingdom: and there shall be famines, and pestilences, and earthquakes, in divers places.*

Fear of Enemies: ***Psalms 118:6*** *The LORD is on my side; I will not fear: what can man do unto me?*

Fear of Slander: ***Psalms 55:3*** *Because of the voice of the enemy, because of the oppression of the wicked: for they cast iniquity upon me, and in wrath they hate me.*

Fear of Darkness: ***Song of Solomon 3:8*** *They all hold swords, being expert in war: every man hath his sword upon his thigh because of fear in the night.*

Fear of Ghosts and Spirits: ***Matthew 14:26*** *And when the disciples saw him walking on the sea, they were troubled, saying, It is a spirit; and they cried out for fear.*

Fear of Facial Expression: ***Jeremiah 1:8*** *Be not afraid of their faces: for I am with thee to deliver thee, saith the LORD.*

Fear of Verbal Rejection and
Fear of Reproach: - ***Isaiah 51:7*** *Hearken unto me, ye that know righteousness, the people in whose heart is my law; fear ye not the reproach of men, neither be ye afraid of their revilings.* (Reproach is rejection, blame, shameful correction or "put downs.")

Fear of Angels:
Matthew 28:4 *And for fear of him the keepers did shake, and became as dead men.*
Luke 1:12 *And when Zacharias saw him, he was troubled, and fear fell upon him.*

Ministry Outline

Prayers of Deliverance

Prayer of Repentance

1. Jesus said: ..*Whatsoever ye shall ask the Father in my name, he will give it you. (John 16:23)* Let us **address our prayer of repentance to our Father in the name of Jesus**.

2. David gave us a beautiful example of a prayer of repentance in Psalm 51: *Have mercy upon me, O God, according to thy lovingkindness: according unto the multitude of thy tender mercies blot out my transgressions. (Psa 51:1)* **Repent and renounce (Name each fear individually).**

3. *Wash me thoroughly from mine iniquity, and cleanse me from my sin. For I acknowledge my transgressions: and my sin is ever before me. (Psalms 51:2,3) Behold, I was shapen in iniquity, and in sin did my mother conceive me. (Psalms 51:5)* **Take responsibility for (Name each fear individually) for all your generations back to Adam and Eve.**

4. **Ask for forgiveness and that the curse be broken.**

A Prayer of Deliverance

In the name of Jesus and by the power of the Holy Spirit, I take authority over (Name each fear individually). I break the power of (Name each fear individually). I cast out (Name each fear individually).

Ministry Outline

Spirits of Fear

Although spirits of fear initially attack us through our spirit man, their realm of influence and support can come from the body (physical), soul (mind, will, emotions), or spirit. Often their influence crosses different areas. Thus, while the following table attempts to classify each by their main realm of influence, remember that they are not exclusive to any one area. As the Holy Spirit leads, add your own revealed fears. Then, renounce and repent for each spirit that you or your forefathers entertained.

Spiritual

Fear of deliverance
Fearful dreams and visions during sleep
Fear of the enemy
Fear of evil spirits
Fear of faith (counterfeit works-faith)
Fear of fear
Fear of God - negative (i.e. being afraid of God)
Fear of Holy Spirit
Fear of judgment
Fear of losing salvation
Fear of man
Fear of night terror/torment (awake or asleep)
Fear of nothing
Fear of not being delivered
Fear of the power of evil
Fear of prophecy
Fear of punishment
Fear of superstitions
Fear to trust in God
Fear of tongues

Physical

Fear of aging
Fear of allergic reactions
Fear of antigens
Fear of chemicals
Cowardice
Fear of death
Fear of disfiguration
Fear of disability
Fear of doctors/hospitals
Fear of drowning
Fear of the dying process

Physical (con't)

Fear of fires
Fear of germs
Fear of heart attack
Fear of illness/disease
Fear of injury
Fear of losing life
Fear of lack
Fear of menopause
Fear of natural disasters
Fear of needles
Fear of not having or not having enough of life's necessities
Fear of poverty
Fear of noises
Fear of pregnancy
Fear of pain
Fear of rape
Fear of robbery
Fear of physical suffering
Fear of steps
Fear of suffocation
Fear of thunder/lightning
Fear of trembling
Fear of war/conflict
Fear of water
Fear of weapons

Senses/Experience

Dread - projection of evil into the future
Fear of change
Fear of dirt
Fear of distress
Fear of independence
Fear of loss of confidence
Fear of loss
Fear of loss of life (wasted years)
Phobias, e.g. claustrophobia
Speculative fear
Stress, worry and anxiety
Fear of vomiting
Fear of unknown

Mind/Mental

Fear of animals
Fear of bad news
Fear of blood
Fear of environment/food/drink/clothes/housing
Fear of the dark
Fear of driving
"Driven-ness"
Fear of dying prematurely
Fear of falling
Fearfulness
Horror
Fear of identity loss
Inferiority
Fear of insanity
Fear of insects
Fear of plants
Panic attacks
Fear of reptiles
Shyness
Fear of success

Sudden fear
Fear of tomorrow or future

Relational/Protectionism

Fear of abandonment
Fear of abandoning loved ones by death or disease
Fear of another's bitterness
Fear of authority
Fear of being alone
Fear of betrayal
Fear of children
Fear of being controlled
Fear children not saved
Fear of commitment
Fear of criticism
Fear of dependency
Fear of disapproval
Fear of discovery - (being found out)
Fear of divorce
Fear of facial expressions
Fear of failure
Fear of family members
Fear of father/mother
Fear of harassment
Fear of humiliation
Fear of inadequacy
Fear of intimacy
Fear of loneliness
Fear of loss of control
Fear of loss of relationship
Fear of loss of spouse
Fear of losing children
Fear of not being loved
Fear of not being able to love
Fear of not meeting expectations
Fear of man
Fear of marriage
Fear of pastors
Perfectionism
Fear of public speaking/ performance
Fear of races/cultures - bigotry
Fear of rejection
Fear of reproach – (being shamed)
Fear of reproof
Fear of responsibility
Self-consciousness
Fear of sex or loss of it
Fear of own sexuality
Fear of another's sexuality
Fear of spouse
Suspicion
Fear of verbal rejection
Fear of another's words

Contributing Source:
"For My Life" Teaching Material
by Henry W. Wright
Pleasant Valley Publications
4178 Highway 74 West
Thomaston, Georgia 30286
Ph: 1 -800-453-5775

Notes

Notes

Notes

Notes

Notes

Notes

Select Teaching Tapes
by Randy Schroeder

1. Four Levels of Hebraic Understanding – The Word of God contains four levels of understanding. Knowing how God and son speak will help enlighten your comprehension of the Word. 2 tapes - $9

2. Understanding Sabbath – Gateway to Freedom - What does the Word say about Sabbath? Who and why was Sabbath changed from the "Jewish" Sabbath to the first day of the week? When and How is Christianity supposed to observe it? This is a teaching that every Christian should consider. 1 tape - $5

3. The Kingdom of God – A teaching on multiple aspects of the kingdom of God. 1 tape - $5

4. The Doctrine of Grace – "God's mercy endures forever," but has liberal teaching distorted the true gift of God's grace? This teaching will put the Word in the sobering light of contextual understanding to show the Body of Christ our responsibility in abiding in it. 1 tape - $5

5. YHVH's Accounting System – For Righteousness – The scriptures speak about three kinds of righteousness; Adamic, Imputed, and the righteousness of Christ. Since Christians have the righteousness of Christ, what importance are imputed and Adamic righteousness to our lives and eternal salvation? 1 tape - $5

6. The "Rapture" (Resurrection) Of The Saints – A Hebraic perspective on what the scriptures say on this controversial subject. 1 tape - $5

7. The Weapons of Our Warfare – Revelations on our spiritual weapons. This two-tape series is a "must" to learn how to put them on. 2 tapes -$10

8. The Walk of Life (The Way, Truth & Life) – Jesus declared that He is the way, the truth and the life. Learn how to stay on the pathway He prepared for us and the simplicity, yet deep revelation of these words. 1 tape -$5

9. This Is Your Life – A study of the books of Ezra and Nehemiah. This is a revolutionary but practical teaching of how to build our own holy temples and walls of defense. Nehemiah, a type of Holy Spirit reveals the defense strategy against the strongman that battles the will of God in our lives. This attractive 8 tape album contains related diagrams. 8 tapes $ 45

Order Form

Gateway to Freedom Publications
P.O. Box 530143
Livonia, MI 48153-0143

Please Print

NAME ______________________________

STREET ______________________________

CITY ____________ **STATE** ______ **ZIP** ______

Quantity	Title	Price
	Overcoming the Fears Within - $12.95 each	
	Three or more books - $11.00 each	
	Subtotal	
	Postage and packaging (see chart below)	
	Total	

Postage and Packaging Rates

# Books	Shipping Method	Cost
1	First Class	$ 2.00
2 – 4	First Class or Priority	$ 4.00
5 –10	Media Mail	$ 4.00

All tape orders include Postage and handling.

http://www.gatewaytofreedom.org

About the Author

Randy Schroeder served as a youth leader (AWANA Commander), teacher, deacon and missionary while he worked in the advertising and marketing business for more than thirty years. Randy was called into full time ministry in 1998 after being ordained under the International Ministers Forum. He and his wife founded Gateway to Freedom, an in-home based ministry in Michigan. The author currently resides in Farmington Hills, Michigan.

Coming Soon

The Rancher and the White Stallion

The Rancher and the White Stallion is the delightful children's story of a wild stallion, named Bright Star and a rancher who loves him. In the story of Bright Star we find the story of the believer's walk beginning outside the ranchers' kingdom, but becoming the faithful and loved servant. Written for children and parents alike, The Rancher and the White Stallion contains a forward explanation for parents and grandparents to teach the principles of receiving and walking with the Master.